DEADLY RUSE

Sands said, "Damn you for a helpless fool, St. Cloud!" His thumb settled on the hammer, ready to pull it back.

"You're yellow," St. Cloud taunted. "Enever knows you're yellow." And then he said it as plainly as it could be said, without telling Sands. "If Enever made a pass at his gun, you'd drop that iron, Sands. You're too yellow to shoot."

Sands' eyes were a blazing fury.

It was then that Enever acted. His hand was hanging at his side. He streaked it up, picking his gun up on the way, and when it was a little more than hip high, he let it off.

Books by Luke Short

AMBUSH
BOLD RIDER
BOUGHT WITH A GUN
BOUNTY GUNS
BRAND OF EMPIRE
THE BRANDED MAN
DESERT CROSSING
THE DESERTERS
DONOVAN'S GUN
THE FEUD AT SINGLE SHOT
FIRST CAMPAIGN
GUNMAN'S CHANCE
THE GUNS OF HANGING
  LAKE
HARD MONEY
HARDCASE
HIGH VERMILION
KING COLT
LAST HUNT
THE MAN FROM TWO
  RIVERS

THE MAN ON THE BLUE
MARAUDERS' MOON
THE OUTRIDER
PAPER SHERIFF
RAIDERS OF THE
  RIMROCK
RAMROD
RAW LAND
RIDE THE MAN DOWN
SAVAGE RANGE
SILVER ROCK
THE SOME-DAY
  COUNTRY
THE STALKERS
STATION WEST
SUMMER OF THE SMOKE
SUNSET GRAZE
THREE FOR THE MONEY
TROUBLE COUNTRY
VENGEANCE VALLEY
THE WHIP

RAIDERS OF THE RIMROCK

Luke Short

A DELL BOOK

Published by
Dell Publishing
a division of
Bantam Doubleday Dell Publishing Group, Inc.
666 Fifth Avenue
New York, New York 10103

ISBN: 0-440-20954-4

Reprinted by arrangement with The Frederick D. Glidden Estate

Printed in the United States of America

Published simultaneously in Canada

October 1991

10 9 8 7 6 5 4 3 2 1

RAD

RAIDERS OF
THE RIMROCK

1

The hotel clerk was puzzled and a little wary of this stranger on the other side of the counter. It wasn't his looks, for they were pleasant enough—far more pleasant, in fact, than the clerk was used to. Nor was it his presence, some six feet of big-boned, saddle-leaned grace. It was his stubbornness, his good-natured, steely-polite insistence, couched in a gentle, deep-Texas drawl. It was the sixth time in as many hours that the clerk had faced it.

"About this Sheriff Borden," Tim Enever said, his watchful gray eyes on the clerk. "He been in after me?"

"Look," the clerk said patiently. "You asked me that this noon. You asked me three times this afternoon. You asked me once before supper and now you ask again." His voice was edged with asperity. "Ain't you Texas men ever heard a man say 'no'?"

"He was supposed to meet me here today," Tim said gently.

"Sure. Only why blame me if he don't?"

"You don't know where he is?"

"Mister, I've had a kid combin' this whole town over for six hours. He can't find him."

"That's funny," Tim drawled stubbornly. "His office is right across the street. Seems like you'd of seen him go in or come out."

The clerk, a middle-aged man, not yet reconciled to his dyspepsia, made an inarticulate gesture. "Why pick on me?" he complained. "There's other people in this town. It ain't my business to keep watch on Borden. I ain't his keeper."

Tim Enever smiled suddenly. It was a quick smile,

friendly, melting the clerk's resentment. "It ain't that. You're the only hombre in town that will talk with a stranger. I asked for Borden in one of the saloons and the bartender went downstairs to look for some beer. I asked in a restaurant and the waiter went back into the kitchen. I asked in a store and the clerk went back into the office." He paused; his tanned face, weather scoured at the prominent cheekbones, was grave, thoughtful, observant. "Don't anybody want to admit they know Borden?"

"Some don't," the clerk said carefully.

"What about you? You ain't afraid to. Why not?"

The clerk said, "Son, I straddle a mighty good fence. Let's let it go at that. I don't know where Borden is. I'm tryin' to find him, and I can't. But I've found his deputy. He'll be over in five minutes, if you want to talk with him."

"I guess I got to," Tim Enever said. "Gimme my key. Room ten. And send this deputy up, will you?"

He accepted his key and took to the stairs just to the right of the desk. He climbed them with a stiff gait, token of a week in the saddle. He was whistling softly in an off-key way that sounded almost lighthearted. It served to cover up a good deal of puzzlement, however, for Tim Enever was troubled. He didn't like this town of Morgan Tanks, didn't like the people in it. Walking its deserted main street at night, a man had the feeling that he'd like to put his back against a wall and take a good look at the shadows across the street. Nobody talked more than necessary. Stores were deserted, and the long tie rails held only an occasional pony, never a buckboard or a spring wagon. That seemed to hint that if a quick getaway was necessary, a buckboard or a wagon was too slow. When a man finished a drink in a saloon he faded out the back door, avoiding the street. And lastly, everybody seemed disinclined to discuss the sheriff.

At the door of room ten, Tim inserted his key and discovered that the door was already unlocked. He pushed inside, fumbled for and found a match in his pants' pocket, whipped it across his seat and started for the lamp on the bureau. His foot caught on something on the floor and he almost stumbled. Recovering himself, he looked down.

A man was lying there on his back, and the flare of the match was reflected by something on his chest. He knelt and brought the match closer. It was a middle-aged, tired-looking man; he had a knife in his throat, and the blood from the wound was pooled around his head. On his vest reposed the star of the sheriff's office.

He had a fighter's face, relaxed now in death, so that the seams of his lined face were almost smooth.

The match died and Tim knelt there, his heart pounding. This man was Sheriff Borden. Even while he was thinking this he heard footsteps on the stairs. A man was mounting them, turning down the corridor toward this room.

Swiftly, without thinking, Tim stood up, closed the door, locked it and then waited in silence. The deputy was about to call on him, and he would find him alone in a room with the dead body of Sheriff Borden. It was a neat frame-up, Tim admitted bitterly—a little too neat, a little too well timed. But by whom?

He tiptoed over to the window and looked out onto the long wooden awning that stretched across the front of the hotel. When the knock came on the door Tim stood motionless. It was repeated firmly, then the handle was tried. Soon the steps retreated as they had come.

Tim had come to a decision. In a very few minutes the clerk was liable to return with a passkey and discover the body. Tim moved swiftly in the dark, sure of himself now. He picked up his war bag, stuffed in it the dirty shirt that hung over the bed. Then he took his razor from the washstand, tucked it in his pocket and dumped the slop water out on the awning roof. Finally, he straightened the spread on the bed, rammed the used towel in his pocket, took the key from the door and stepped out the open window onto the awning.

The window of the adjoining room was unlocked, and with a prayer that he would find it unoccupied, Tim hoisted the window and climbed in. He struck a match, and breathed a sigh of relief at finding the room empty. Swiftly, he set about mussing up the room. He tramped on the spread, scattered some clothes from his war bag about the room, poured water in the basin, splashed some on the floor, and put his razor on the washstand. After crumpling a towel, he went to the door and opened it.

The way was still clear. He tiptoed down to the L in the corridor by the stairs, and hid himself just as the sound of two men climbing the stairs ascended the stair well.

He heard a bass voice say, "You're sure it's ten, George!"

"I never forgot a room number in my life." This was the clerk's voice. "I know he's there. He went up not three minutes before you come."

"Well, he must be damn sleepy," the other observed.

Tim waited until they reached the landing and went down the corridor, then he dodged down the stairs—— From the angle in it, he could reach the board where the room keys hung. He exchanged the key to room ten for the key to room eleven and mounted the stairs again.

The light in room ten cast its beam out into the dimly lighted hall. Tim sidled up to the door and leaned on its jamb. It was a minute before the clerk, staring at the body in startled horror, looked up and saw him.

"There he is!" he cried, almost dropping the lamp he held.

The deputy, who had been kneeling over the body of Sheriff Borden, rose, and in one swift motion drew his gun, wheeling to face Tim.

Tim didn't move, only looked at the gun and then at Sheriff Borden's body, mild surprise on his face.

"Dead man, hunh?" he asked innocently.

"You ought to know," the deputy said, after a pregnant pause. "You killed him." He was a burly man with a square, heavily fleshed face. His clothes, of town variety, were unpressed and careless looking, but Tim took the trouble to notice that he wore two holsters under the skirt of his coat.

His face had the cast of a cross-grained man, crafty and implacably stubborn where the line of the jaw rose above his opened collar.

"Did I, now?" Tim drawled easily. "What for, do you reckon?"

"Mister, this is your room," the deputy began. "We found him in——"

"Wait a minute," Tim cut in. "This ain't my room, so that's out to begin with. What else?"

"Your room's ten," the clerk said quickly. "This is room ten."

"This is ten, right enough, but my room's eleven," Tim observed. He jerked a thumb toward the next room. "Have a look, if you don't believe me."

"I'll do that," the deputy said. Tim unlocked the door to his room, lighted the lamp under the gun of the deputy and stood aside for them to observe the room. The bed was mussed; clothes were strewn over the floor; there was a razor on the washstand, and the towel was used. It looked convincing even to Tim.

"But your room is ten!" the clerk insisted.

Tim held out his key. "What am I doin' with this, then?"

The key was to room eleven. The clerk looked at the deputy and shook his head. Tim watched the deputy, but the man's face betrayed only a mild surprise. With his free hand the deputy lifted his hat and scratched his hair. It was a piebald color, a blond gray, shading into chestnut and streaked in two or three places with white. He looked at the clerk with heavy disapproval.

"Make up your mind, Shelley. Is it room ten or eleven?"

"Ten!" the clerk snapped. "I tell you I never made a mistake in remembering room numbers in my life. It's ten."

The deputy snorted and looked cautiously at Tim. "You deny you been lookin' for Sheriff Borden all day?"

"No. Half a day, if you want to be accurate."

"What for?"

"I heard he was sellin' Christmas toys," Tim drawled

innocently. "They told me he had a prize collection of tin horns in the sheriff's office."

The deputy's face flushed, and he looked as if he were going to choke. If Tim had ever had the idea that he would confess his business to Sheriff Borden's deputy he had changed his mind. The man was a blundering, suspicious fool; that he might be crooked in the bargain, Tim was not yet sure.

The deputy said, "I think I'll hold you, mister."

"And I reckon you won't," Tim said gently.

"And I reckon the same," a third voice put in from the corridor. It was a firm voice, edged with iron.

Tim turned to behold a tall, white-haired man in a suit of black broadcloth. A pair of dead-white saber mustaches bisected his narrow face, disclosing a sharp deeply cleft chin below, and above a thin nose and predatory black eyes. There was a quiet arrogance in his look, his manner and his speech that put any man to a disadvantage. He looked straight at the deputy, the mockery in his dark eyes a quiet challenge.

"I couldn't help but overhear this from my room," the stranger said. "Mersey, you're a complete fool."

"Keep out of this, Sands," the deputy warned ominously.

"I intend to—after I've seen elementary justice done," Sands said evenly. "I've been in my room all evening. I haven't heard a scuffle of any sort. I heard this man come in about ten minutes ago—and he went into room eleven."

"I suppose you could see that through a closed door," Mersey sneered.

"I didn't need to," the older man answered. "If you'll try this door you'll know that it squeaks when it's opened. His door did not squeak when it was opened."

The deputy's eyes grew crafty. "How'd you know it squeaked if you'd never heard him open it?"

Sands smiled pityingly. "You forget. I heard you open it, my friend." His smile remained as the deputy's beefy face relaxed in confusion. He went on, "I also happen to know that he hasn't been in his room up till ten minutes ago. Now if you can name the time of the murder, the motive, the evidence against the man, and show a possible way he could have done it without my hearing, then I'll begin to believe that you're clever instead of just clumsy, Mersey."

The deputy did not lower his gun. "In this county, Sands, it takes more than the word of a sheepman to swing a jury."

Sands still smiled. "Want to prove that, Will? If you do let's take it to court. I'll fight it up to the Supreme Court. And there, I believe, you'll find men who are more interested in justice than in sheep or cattle. I repeat, do you want to take the case to court?"

Tim smothered a smile. These two had forgotten him. This Sands did not know him, yet in the course of five minutes had offered to fight his case clear to the Supreme Court.

The deputy now holstered his gun. "We can't fight your money, Sands," he sneered. "It strikes me that you're just contrary enough to spend fifty thousand dollars to prove this office is wrong."

"Correct," Sands said calmly.

The deputy glared at him for three long seconds, then looked at Tim. "I don't know you, mister, but if you stick around this town long enough I aim to."

"And I aim to stick," Tim said quietly.

The deputy nodded curtly and said, "Would you have the damn kindness to clear out of here, you two? The smell of sheep is a little rank."

Sands still smiled gently. He backed out of the doorway into the corridor. Tim followed. The deputy locked the window, came out, waited for the clerk to lock the room and they went down the hall together.

Tim turned to Sands, observing him more carefully. There was a faint look of amusement in the man's eyes.

"I'm obliged," Tim said.

"Come along," Sands said shortly. He opened the door in the opposite wall and led the way into a spacious sitting room. There was a girl standing by the table in front of the window. She gave them a careless glance over her shoulder as they entered, then returned her attention to a book on the table. In that brief second Tim saw only her profile—proud, a little sulky, but as clean and modeled and lovely under the full sweep of her black hair as a cameo.

"Leave us alone, Julie," Sands said briefly.

Without another glance at them, the girl went through a door into an adjoining room and closed it behind her.

Sands walked up to the table, Tim following. Suddenly, Sands turned to face him, and Tim saw swiftly that the man was furious. His lips were drawn back over his teeth, and his eyes seemed to smolder in their sockets.

"You damned fool," he said, his voice husky. "Do you think I'll tolerate as clumsy a job of murder as that?"

2

For a moment Tim could not grasp the implication.

"Do you?" Sands repeated.

"Wait a minute," Tim drawled. "You've got the wrong man."

It was Sands' turn to be puzzled. He stared at Tim, and the anger seemed to fade out of his eyes. He did not speak for a long time, and when he did it was in a controlled voice.

"Gates didn't send you?"

"Gates who?"

"Well, well," Sands said quietly. "It seems I've made a mistake."

"I reckon that's it."

"One that can be corrected in only one way," Sands continued. And then he laughed. "Do you smoke?" he asked easily and reached in his pocket. When his hand came out it was holding a derringer. Moreover, it was a derringer designed to hold a shotgun shell, and it was pointed, cocked, at Tim's midriff.

"My friend," he said quietly, "I don't like to do this. But I don't see any other way out, do you?"

Tim looked up from the derringer to the older man's face, and he felt cold sweat on his temples. "I can think of a lot of ways," he said. "First, I take it, you aimed to have Sheriff Borden killed?"

"That's it."

"And you thought I was the man Gates sent up to do it?"

"Yes."

Tim shrugged. "All right. Borden's dead, I didn't do it, and I reckon if your man did it he got away. So I don't see why you figure you got to blow a hole in me. The only evidence I got against you is that you wanted Borden dead. That won't hold water in court, even if I took it there."

Sands seemed to consider this. Tim shifted his feet faintly, his movement observed by the older man. Tim knew a killer when he saw him, and Sands was a killer. Not the bragging, two-gun kind, but the cold and ruthless kind.

"I don't think I'd better listen any more," Sands said gently. "I've got too much at stake." He smiled mockingly. "You see, I'm about to change this whole Tornado Basin from a cattle range into sheep country. I can't afford mistakes."

"It'll make a hell of a noise," Tim said, stalling desperately for time.

"I won't try to hide it," Sands said. "I'll tell Will Mersey you're Borden's killer."

"That girl. She'll know the truth."

"She's my daughter," Sands said. "She knows a daughter's duty."

"Then she forgot it," Tim lied blandly, "when she stopped me down in the lobby."

Sands' face changed imperceptibly. "Stopped you? When?"

"This noon."

"What for?"

"To ask me if I could get a horse for her tonight after you'd gone to bed."

"You lie!" Sands said, but he wasn't convinced.

"All you got to do is back off, holdin' that gun on me, and look out the window onto the alley. There's a horse I got her, tied to the woodshed. All you got to do is reach in my pocket for the hundred dollars she give me."

It was a desperate gamble, Tim knew, and for a moment he couldn't see how it would work. But it was the thin edge of the wedge, a suspicion planted, and after ten long seconds Tim knew that it had taken root. He could read it on Sands' face. Sands knew he was lying—almost—but he couldn't be sure.

Sands said coldly, "If there's not a horse down there in plain sight, I'll blow a hole a foot wide in your chest."

"He's down there all right," Tim said serenely. He watched breathlessly while Sands backed carefully to the end of the table, around it, and put a hand on the curtain.

"If you make a move I'll let go," Sands said calmly.

"Sure you will. Only you won't shoot before you see whether there's a horse down there. Because if you do you'll never be quite sure whether Julie's against you or for you."

Sands looked at him a long moment, indecision in his face. Then he took a deep breath, and swiftly turned his head. Tim didn't make a move, because he knew Sands wouldn't risk a long look at first. And sure enough, Sands turned his head back almost immediately.

"You lie!" he said.

"You look," Tim said serenely. "Just give your eyes time the next look."

Again Sands seemed undecided. Then, as if making up his mind, he straightened up and swiveled his head, his face full at the window.

Tim melted to the floor and rolled toward the table, just as the blast rocked the room. He felt something rake his back, like a claw, and then he made a wild lunge for Sands' boots. He got a foot and twisted savagely. He felt a crushing blow on his shoulder, and knew that it was the derringer which Sands aimed for his head. Sands crashed to the floor, and Tim was on him. Two vicious slugs, a left and a right, into that lean face and Sands relaxed.

Tim leaped to his feet, and found the girl standing in the doorway. "Did you kill him?" she asked calmly.

"No, ma'am. And I'll never understand why I didn't," Tim growled.

"You'd better get out of here," Julie said swiftly. "He had his men in rooms on both sides."

The sound of running feet echoed in the hallway.

"Quick," Julie said, beckoning him into her room. He brushed past her and she closed and locked her door, then raced for the window.

Tim helped her raise it. The night outside was utterly black, unrelieved by a glimmer of light anywhere.

"There's a shed roof ten feet below," Julie said.

Tim looked out. He couldn't see it. He turned to her. "You sure?"

"Positive. It slopes toward the back alley, and then there's a pile of wood beneath it. You could jump on the wood and then to the ground."

Tim looked at her. Her blue eyes were bright with excitement, and the sulkiness had left her face. Someone started pounding on the door and calling, "Miss Julie! Miss Julie!"

Tim nodded and said, "Thanks," and swung himself out of the window, holding onto the sill with his hands. His feet did not touch. If she was lying he would have two broken legs within the next ten seconds. He looked up at her, and saw the faint smile of excitement on her face, and then he let go.

Abruptly, after a four-foot fall, he landed on the shed roof. He started to slide immediately, and braced himself as best he could. He made a grab for the edge of the roof, but his grip broke and again he was falling. This fall was shorter, and he landed in a tangle of short lengths of fire-wood. A volley of shots burst out above him, drumming into the shed roof. He scrambled down the woodpile, cursing the noise he made, and ducked toward the street. He glanced over his shoulder once, and saw two men framed in the window of the girl's room, peering foolishly out into the night, guns in hand.

At the livery stable which faced Morgan Tanks' single darkened street a block below the Stockman's House, he found an old hostler seated in the archway of the stable, a lantern over his head.

Tim shucked out two gold coins and tossed them into the man's lap and said, "I want three questions answered, and I want the truth. Is that enough?"

"More 'n enough," the old man said deliberately.

"All right. One: Is there an honest cattleman in this county?"

"Jeff Hardy, at the Ox-Bow."

"Where is it?"

"Six hours' ride out the north road. Take every right-hand road and you can't miss it."

Tim wheeled and headed back for the stalls. "Wait a minute," the hostler said. "You got one more question comin'."

"You've answered it," Tim said grimly. "I was goin' to ask how long it would take me to get there."

It took him a little more than six hours, as it turned out. He was glad enough of the extra time, for he wanted to puzzle out several things. The man Sands was transparent; he appeared to be a shrewd and ruthless man, backed by a lot of money and doubtless men, who was going to take over a cattle range for sheep. That he dared to live in a hotel in the midst of cattlemen attested to his power. His daughter was a different story. Tim couldn't help but remember how she had asked, "Did you kill him?" without a trace of horror, of anger or of dread. And she had helped him escape, further proof that she didn't sympathize with her father.

And Sands knew it, or he wouldn't have been so gullible about the horse.

But what really troubled Tim was the deputy, Will Mersey. In any questioning, there is usually right and wrong, good men and bad. There was a right in this case, the cowman's right. But the only cattleman Tim had met was Will Mersey, a blundering fool. There was nothing much right about him. It troubled Tim, because he had already chosen his side in this fight. But it made him wonder what kind of a man Sheriff Borden had been, and what kind of men the other cattlemen were. He was soon to see.

The Ox-Bow, in the light of a quarter moon, lay in a shallow valley backed by the foothills of the Tornadoes that rose to tower in dim snow-capped aloofness to the north and east. Timber crawled down from the foothills to fringe the house at the rear. The house itself was of rock construction, two-story in the main part, and flanked by single-story wings of timber. The lights, except for those in the bunkhouse between the house and the clutter of corrals and barns, were centered in the main house. Tim rode for them, announcing his entrance by the racket his sorrel kicked up when he crossed the timber bridge over the stream.

A huge live oak shaded the front yard. Tim pulled up beside it, and waited for the inevitable challenge, which came from a corner of the porch.

"Who are you?" a quiet voice asked.

"I've got news for Jeff Hardy," Tim said, making no attempt to dismount.

"What kind of news?"

"Sheriff Borden has just been murdered," Tim drawled.

There was a long silence, and then a shape appeared out of the dark. It was a puncher.

"What did you say?" he asked.

Tim repeated it. The man said, "Get down and reach for it." When Tim was dismounted he was relieved of his guns and the barrel of a Colt .44 was placed in the small of his back. "Up the steps and in the house," the man said.

Tim marched onto the porch and through the door, which was open against the warm evening. The hall let immediately onto a lighted room, and Tim stopped in the doorway of it.

Smoke lay in ragged banners in the V of light cast below and above the lamp on the table in the room's center. There were many men here, Tim could see. He had stumbled onto some sort of meeting, for there was a figure leaning against the mantel of the cold fireplace at the end of the room. He looked at this figure and was about to look away when his glance returned to it. It was a woman, dressed in men's jeans and jumper. Evidently, she had been talking when interrupted by his entrance. She regarded him quietly, and all Tim could see of her in that half dusk was a mass of tawny hair framing a slim and young face.

"Yes, George," one of the men said. He was sitting next to the fireplace in a deep chair. Even in that attitude, Tim could see that he was a giant of a man, and very, very old. His skin was dry and looked brittle, and his hands, just edging into the direct light of the lamp, were twisted and veined and thick fingered. His voice was a low and tired rumble.

"This gent rode up and said Borden's been killed," the puncher announced flatly.

Something stirred through the room. You could tell these men had talked themselves out and were sitting in weary lethargy. But this news seemed to wake them—or half of them, that is. For against the east wall were men of a type—poor men, over-worked and saddle gaunted men—whose clothes and guns showed their poverty. Against the west wall were more solid-looking men. They were cleaner, their boots were tooled, and their guns were pearl and ivory handled.

It was the poor men, the ones against the east wall, who seemed moved by this news. One of them rose slowly to his feet and said, "You say Borden was murdered?"

"Murdered in my room at the Stockman's House to-night," Tim repeated. "A knife in his throat."

The gaunted nester said nothing for three seconds, then he murmured, "God help us poor nesters, now that Borden's dead."

There was a long silence among the more affluent ranchers, as if each man of them wanted to weigh this news against his own personal fortunes. And it was obvious to Tim that the news of Borden's death did not move them. It was the girl who spoke next.

"Well, nester or big rancher, we've waited too long. Sands got to Borden while we were wrangling."

"I don't think so," Tim cut in quietly. He told them of the whole business there at the hotel, and of how Sands saved him, only to turn on him later. "He didn't kill Borden. He didn't have him killed. He was goin' to but he didn't."

The girl hung on his every word. While Tim was talking he had watched her more than the others. She was thin and there were shadowed spots under her eyes, as if she were burdened with something beyond her power to carry. But it was the look in her face, something that was pride and not arrogance in her full mouth, something that was worry but not defeat in her deep brown eyes, that drew Tim's glance back to her time and again.

When he had finished she said, "Then who did kill him?"

"Maybe," a thin voice said, "we're lookin' at him."

Tim wheeled to see the speaker. He was one of a dozen shabbily dressed men on the benches lining the east wall of the room. He had not shaved in a week; he held a cud of tobacco pouched in his cheek, and there was a kind of insolent shiftiness to his watery eyes.

"I took that once tonight," Tim drawled, anger edging his voice. "I don't aim to do it again."

"Don't see how you can help it," the man retorted, his voice rising.

"You want me to show you?"

"I'd admire to have you."

Tim took a swift step toward the man, who scrambled to his feet, clawing at the gun in his belt.

"Stop!" a voice commanded. It was the girl's. "In heaven's name, Wiley, sit down! And you, stranger, you're touchier than the whole lot of us!"

Tim relaxed slowly and turned toward the girl. "I'm a cowman," he said gently, his gray eyes sultry. "But tonight I haven't seen much in the way of cowmen that make me proud. I got cuffed around by a loudmouth deputy there in town, and I get pushed around by an out-at-the-pants saddle bum out here. You reckon I should sing about it?"

"I think you'd better watch your tongue," the girl said calmly.

But there was an end to patience, and Tim had arrived there. "I come here to try and help you. But to hell with that! Hell with the lot of you! If you think you can stop me from ridin' off this place, then cut loose your dogs, because I'm leavin'."

The first one to move was the girl. She came around the table and stood up to Tim, and her face was taut with worry. "Please, please, don't go! If I was sharp I'm sorry. But all our nerves are on edge. Do you blame us for being suspicious when a perfect stranger tells us our sheriff has been killed?"

The old man in the chair, who had been silent up to now, said in a kindly voice, "We're folks, son. Sit down and cool off and tell us who you are."

Tim relaxed. He felt a little sheepish now, but his resentment was not entirely conquered. "Tim Enever's son," he said quietly. "Borden wrote the Cattle Association office a month ago, and asked for a man out here. Said trouble was buildin' up faster 'n he could take care of it. I rode into town today, and I couldn't find Borden. Since then, I've had a sheepman take a shot at me, and cowmen cuss me. I don't like it."

Wiley spoke up again. "If even Borden reckoned we'd pay

for a damn range detective he was wrong. I ain't puttin' in a cent to this man's wages."

"For me," one of the big ranchers against the west wall said emphatically. "It sounds like a dumb nester-sheriff's plan."

The girl caught Tim's eye. She smiled faintly, hopelessly, and shrugged, as if to say, "You see, I'm doing my best to keep peace, but it's impossible."

Tim said abruptly. "Don't worry about that. I don't expect pay. All I'm askin' for is a chance at a man who holds a shotgun derringer in my belly and tells me he'll blow a hole in me."

The girl looked grateful. The old man chuckled and said, "There's one man on your side, Martha."

The girl nodded wearily. "Yes. That's two of us." She looked around at the group of men. "Well, why don't you go home? What are you staying for? It's late—and nothing is settled."

Wiley rose and said lazily, "Just curiosity, I reckon." He looked slyly at Martha. "You oughta had more sense, Miss Kincaid, than try to make nesters and big ranchers lie down in the same bed. It can't be did. As long as Maury Borden was alive, we poor people knew we'd get some kind of justice. But now that he's dead, I dunno but what I'll take sheep to the kind of rich neighbors I got."

"Go ahead and take 'em," the same big rancher said shortly. He was a man of medium size, heavy of jowl, determined looking. He had a hard time controlling his voice. "There ain't an honest cattleman in the whole lot of you squatters. Swing over to sheep. I'd as soon fight you in the open as claim you for a friend while my cattle disappeared."

Martha Kincaid had given up hope. You could see it in her face. "All right, Lugan," she said to the big rancher. "Let it ride that way. You'd rather fight us nesters than the sheepmen, than Sands, and it looks like we'd rather fight you than Sands, too. But not me. I say we band together or we go down. Remember that, the last of you who are alive when the woollies are eating Tornado Basin into a desert. Remember that when Sands moves across the river with his hired gunmen. Remember that you'd rather fight between yourselves than fight a common enemy." She laughed bitterly. "Pleasant dreams, you Mexican generals. I'm going out and be sick."

She stalked out of the room amid utter silence. Only old Jeff Hardy in his deep chair made a noise. He laughed.

3

Before Tim could join the crew for breakfast in the cookshack next morning, he was summoned to the main house. Old Jeff Hardy sat in the kitchen, a cup of coffee before him on the table. Tim's breakfast was being laid out by a Chinese cook. Jeff Hardy gestured to the table and said, "I've eaten. Go ahead."

Tim tied into breakfast while the old man smoked his pipe and regarded the stranger from under shaggy brows. There was something peaceful and big and waiting about old man Jeff Hardy; he looked at the world from deep blue eyes and said nothing.

When Tim was finished he rolled a smoke and pushed back his chair. There was much he wanted to talk about. Last night old Jeff had stalked out of the room with a bare good night for him, and George had taken him to the bunkhouse. This morning it looked as if old man Hardy was going to talk.

And he did. He said, "What do you think of this damn rabble we call cowmen here?"

"Not much," Tim said.

Old Jeff smiled. "I trapped all the grizzlies in this Basin, son. I fought the Indians till they was sick of me. I lived here for fifty-odd years, and some of that time it was seven hundred miles to the nearest store. I tamed this country—makin' it ready for this tripe of cowmen."

"Makin' it ready for sheepmen, you mean," Tim said.

Old Jeff nodded. "That's right."

"What will you do about that?"

"Do? Why, hell, I'll fight. I'll die with my boots on, shootin' at sheepmen. A man couldn't ask for a finer death, could he?"

"Not if you're ready to go," Tim conceded.

"I am. I've raised eight boys and sent 'em away. They've raised boys, too, and those boys have raised boys. I can still smoke, still drink enough to warm my belly, and I can still ride." He paused, his lined face in repose. "And I can whip hell out of my neighbors, if I've a mind to. And sometimes I think I've a mind to."

Tim smiled faintly and said nothing.

"Only trouble is," Jeff went on, "if they go down, she goes down. And I don't like that."

"She?"

"Martha Kincaid. She's worth the pack of 'em. She's got twice their guts, five times their brains and a thousand times their looks when worry ain't ridin' hell out of her."

"She's tired," Tim said softly. "A man could see that."

"Tired to death," Jeff agreed. "She's done a lot, but not enough. I never thought she could do that much."

"How much?"

Old Jeff crossed his legs. He did not help those old legs with his hands; they worked of themselves. "Two months ago," Jeff said slowly, "Wiley and Lugan would've shot at each other on sight."

"They came close to it last night."

"I know. But they was in the same room. They talked. They listened—even if they didn't agree. There was six-seven rich men and twelve poor men in that room—something I never thought I'd see."

"And why not?" Tim asked.

Old Jeff smiled a little. "It's the old story, son. Them that have wants more; them that haven't wants some. The big ranchers hate and fight the nesters, the nesters hate and fight them. Martha Kincaid is a nester's girl. But she's got the brains to see that if us cowmen, big and little, are goin' to drive Sands off, we got to band together. She's workin' night and day to bring it to pass. But she can't do it. Borden was helpin' her, but now that he's gone she ain't got any help."

"I think she has," Tim said quietly.

Old Jeff regarded him a long time. "Yes, I think she has," he murmured. "That's why I took you in."

"What's the best way to do it?" Tim asked.

"There ain't any way. But that's no reason you shouldn't try." Jeff hitched his chair closer. "I'll tell you all I know, and you can have it for what it's worth. Borden was a nester-sheriff, but an honest man. The big ranchers didn't like him, and the nesters loved him. They believed in him. When Sands started movin' his sheep up the other side of the south Tornadoes last summer, Borden knew what was comin'. Sands even told 'em he was comin' over. Borden's job was to hold the nesters together until he could swing the big ranchers in with them to fight Sands and his gunmen. Martha worked with him. It was a fight, for Sands was fightin' with money."

"How?"

"Why, if you was a nester with fifty head of cattle, a piece of bottom land and a shack, and a man come along and offered you three-four thousand dollars for the outfit and title to your claim, wouldn't you sell?"

"Not to a sheepman."

"But you're a cattleman, son, a real one. They ain't. They're just tryin' to live. If they could do it with a hoe better than by raisin' cattle, they'd take to the hoe. They're fightin' for existence—and money is existence."

"I see," Tim said slowly.

"And as long as Borden was alive, they wouldn't sell. But

now he's dead, there's nothin' to stop 'em. They figure they can't fight Sands alone. They'll take his money and clear out."

"How much time have we got?" Tim asked.

"None."

"You mean he's here?"

Old Jeff nodded. "Long ago we decided the river was the line. All the nesters is squatted on the north bank of the river. Yesterday forty thousand head of sheep watered at the river comin' up from the south and east. Today, tomorrow, a week from now, they'll cross. He'll buy out the nesters and get a claim on the north bank. That claim is just as good as ours to all the Tornado Basin open range. After that—war."

Tim stirred restlessly. "I'd like to see Martha Kincaid."

Old Jeff stood up. "I reckoned you would. I'll take you to her."

Riding out of the Ox-Bow, the great mottled expanse of Tornado Basin stretched out before them like a sleek animal sunning its side. Miles and miles of rolling grassland stretched to the west to end against the faint blue ramparts of distant Pipestone Peaks. To the south, it was cut by the river which finally turned south and vanished into the desert, while to the north and east the Tornadoes shouldered cloud high, the guardian peaks.

A long morning's ride put them in sight of a ribbon of green timber which announced the river. Joe Kincaid's holding, Old Jeff said, was the choice one of the nester folk. He had come late, when the grasslands were claimed and backed by armed riders, but he didn't want much. He was sick, his wife was dead, and he was seeking only a home for himself and his little girl. He started honest—that is, he bought his cattle instead of stealing them. And this act bought him toleration from the big ranchers. He had died two years ago, having lived long enough to see his girl a woman. And he had died respected—but a nester. Since then, Joe Kincaid's place had been run by the girl and a crippled Negro puncher.

When Tim saw the place he understood why Martha Kincaid was willing to fight for it. It was off the bottom lands of Tornado River on the shoulder of the low bluff. Built of logs, it was not just another line camp shack slung up for shelter. Nor was it, on the other hand, a pretty place. It looked like a ranch. Its outbuildings and corrals were rough, solid, but its windows had curtains, and there were flowers growing around the door. From the front step many miles of the tree-fringed Tornadoes stretched away in a green ribbon below.

Martha Kincaid met them at the door and bid them dismount and come in. The house was small, neat as a ship's cabin. Martha was wearing a dress of blue calico this morning, and above its open neck Tim could see the deep pockets of her collarbones. She was thin, like a horse trained down too fine.

Old Jeff chose a bench by the door. Tim squatted on his heels against the house and Martha sat on the step.

"Never know when you're licked,—do you, girl?" Old Jeff began.

"I do now, Uncle Jeff," Martha answered. She smiled wearily. "I learned last night."

"Did Curt bring any news about Sands this mornin'?"

"He hasn't moved across yet. Wiley was talking to his foreman today."

"Looks like it's started then, don't it?"

"It does."

Tim said swiftly, "Look here, Miss Kincaid. Isn't there somethin' that will stop men like Wiley from sellin' out?"

"Like what?" Martha asked, turning her troubled gaze full upon him.

Tim frowned. "More money, maybe. Why don't these jugheaded big ranchers get together and buy these nesters out? Pay 'em more than Sands will."

"And buy back what they believe they already own?" Martha said. She shook her head gravely. "They're too proud. No, that's been tried. It's not the way."

Tim was watching her closely. He picked up a handful of gravel and sifted it through his fingers and then said softly, "There is a way. It isn't pretty. But it's a way."

"Scaring them into joining up together, you mean?" Martha asked.

Tim nodded. "What if——"

The sound of an approaching horse cut him short. He looked up to see Lugan, the spokesman for the big ranchers, riding toward them. Lugan waved and Martha waved back, and he came up and dismounted. In the morning light he looked younger, perhaps thirty-five. He was a burly man, not tall, but thick and solid, and his clothes were of the range variety. When he took off his hat his curly chestnut hair glinted in the sun. He nodded pleasantly to Jeff and Tim.

"Hello, John," Martha greeted him. "You're off the reservation, aren't you?"

Lugan grinned. "I had to take a look at the woollies this morning."

"Really," Martha said dryly. "I didn't know you were interested."

Lugan laughed. "That only partly explains why I'm down this way. I came to apologize."

"For being bullheaded?" Martha asked, smiling. "You can't help that, I guess."

"I reckon not," Lugan agreed. "Especially when I don't want to help it. Still, if I said anything last night that offended you, I'm sorry."

"You didn't," Martha said. "If I said anything that offended you, I'm glad of it." Her smile took the sharpness from the words. "You see, if by offending you I can wake you up, John, I'll risk it."

Lugan laughed again. "No use, Martha. You're the only nester I'd touch with a ten-foot pole."

"That's queer. I'm just a human being, trying to live. They are, too."

"But a different kind," Lugan said. He glanced over anxiously at Tim. "Will Mersey's looking for you," he said. "I met him at the turn-off into the Ox-Bow."

"They'll steer him over here," Jeff said serenely. He added, "How did the sheep look? Think they'll thrive on your grass, John?"

"They'll never get there," Lugan said confidently. He touched his hat to Martha, stepped into the saddle and said, "If Sands moves a foot onto your range, Martha, let me know. My crew is at your disposal."

"Thanks, but you'll need them all yourself," Martha replied.

Lugan rode off then, Martha watched him go, her eyes speculative, Tim thought. Then she turned to Tim again. "You were saying something when he rode up, weren't you?"

Tim nodded, wondering how what he would say would sound in the mouth of a stranger. He was looking at Lugan's retreating figure. "Suppose," he said in his mild drawl, "I was to get on my horse and ride after Lugan. He's goin' home. There must be some sort of a gut or a cut bank he'll have to pass. Suppose I had a pocketful of shells and waited at that cut bank for him. Suppose I shot his horse out from under him and threw lead all around him for three-four hours. And then suppose I left a glove, a spur, a hatband, a tuft of wool or something behind me, so that when he came out and tried to figure who's been potshooting at him, he'd find this clue and figure Sands was trying to get him. Suppose I did that to half a dozen ranchers around here. Suppose I burned some of the nesters' barns. And each time it would look like one of Sands' riders had done it." He looked at Martha now. "You reckon they might see how helpless they are workin' alone? You reckon they'd talk it over and decide to gang up for protection?"

Jeff Hardy laughed softly, but Tim paid no attention to him. He was looking at this quiet, passionate girl, and she was looking at him.

"I hoped you'd say that," she said at last. "Maybe you

think I'm ruthless or cruel. I'm not. I don't always believe that the end justifies the means, but I do now. I'd thought of that, but you see, I couldn't do it alone."

"You can't do it all," Tim said. "I can. Give me your man to help me."

"Where will you get the things to plant—the guns, or the hatbands?"

"It won't be the first sheep camp I've ridden into and shot up," Tim said grimly. "I'll take what I want."

"You couldn't."

"I'll tell you after I've tried," Tim said. "I'll do it to-night."

Martha looked at him a long time, something close to tears filming her eyes. Then she said gently, "It's not right. You've nothing at stake. You'll risk your life for a gang of men who aren't worth it."

Tim grinned. "It's my life. And it's not a risk."

Old Jeff Hardy cleared his throat. "There's someone comin'," he announced. Presently, over the brow of the ridge, Will Mersey rode into sight. He pulled up in front of them and tipped his hat to Martha and nodded to Tim.

"You sure do some tall hellity-hootin' around the country for an old man, Jeff," he announced, dismounting lazily.

"When there's a deputy ridin' my tail I always travel," Jeff said. "What is it?"

Will Mersey was sweating in spite of the coolness of the morning, but he seemed at ease. He loafed over to Tim and squatted down in the shade on his heels beside him. "News," he said, cuffing his hat back off his forehead. "Caslon at the bank tells me he's just got word that Sands is goin' to open a bank in Morgan Tanks."

"What of it?" Old Jeff said calmly.

"Caslon wanted you to know, you bein' a director."

"Hell, if he can make any money at it he's welcome," Jeff said. He pulled out his pipe and packed it.

Mersey said, "Well, that's that. It's a long ways to ride to git laughed at."

Tim grinned at him. Mersey seemed to be a cheerful sort of cuss this morning, a little different from last night. They talked idly of the new bank's prospects. During a pause in the conversation, Mersey said, "You know, Martha, I never knew you had a wild-plum thicket so close to you."

"Plums?" Martha said. "Where?"

Mersey pointed lazily toward the river. "Across there beyond that live-oak thicket. Ain't them plums?"

Martha stood up to look across the river. Jeff Hardy turned his head and squinted. Even Tim looked.

As soon as his head was turned Tim felt a gun jammed into his ribs. In one swift second, Mersey lifted his gun from its holster, rose to his feet and backed off.

"Don't make a move, damn you," he said quietly.

Martha whirled to behold Will Mersey pointing two guns at Tim, who was still sitting on the ground. Jeff turned his head, saw, and puffed peacefully on his pipe.

"Why, Will!" Martha said. "What's the matter?"

"Plenty," Will said grimly, never taking his eyes off Tim. "Jeff, I'm sorry I had to run that sandy about the bank. It wasn't true. But I had to make up some excuse so's this hombre wouldn't suspect me."

"Suspect you of what?" Jeff said dryly. "Brains?"

"That's all right," Will said doggedly, his guns leveled. "Laugh at me when I tell you this. I got absolute proof that this ranahan murdered Sheriff Borden."

Tim started to hoist himself to his feet, when Mersey said sharply, "Sit still!"

"All right," Tim said. "But quit shakin'. One of those guns is liable to go off."

"It'd be a good thing if it did," Mersey said.

"Will, what kind of proof have you?" Martha asked in a hushed voice.

"You wouldn't understand it, Martha," Mersey said. "But he will."

He said to Tim, "There was a jasper sittin' in the dark

corner of the lobby when you snaked that key to room eleven off the hook and put the key to ten in its place."

"That's a little thing to hang a man on," Tim murmured. His eyes were not pleasant to look at, and his lips were a little pale.

"It ain't that," the deputy said. "It's what we found in your war bag. You left in a little bit of a hurry."

"What if I did?"

"Shelley, the clerk, brought your stuff over to me this mornin'. I thought I'd look through it." His voice changed a little. "Martha, there's somethin' in my right hip pocket. Take it out, will you? And if you try to knock my guns down I'll shoot him."

"Don't be a fool," Martha said. "Try and keep calm. I won't touch your hands." She crossed over to him and reached in his hip pocket. What she brought out was the sheath for a knife, a sheath made out of soft antelope hide. She looked at it and said, "I don't see the connection between a knife sheath and the murder, Will."

"I found it in his war bag. It fits the knife that was left in Borden's throat. Turn it over."

Martha turned it over. On the hide side, in the faintest of ink, were the initials T. E.

"Is this yours, Tim?" Martha asked.

Tim nodded. "But the knife found in Borden's throat wasn't my knife. It was agate handled."

"Did you have your knife marked?" Mersey asked quietly.

Tim thought a moment. "It was bone handled, a skinning knife. I made it from a file and tempered it. The top edge has a file edge."

"Anything else?"

"Yes. One of the handles was chipped."

"Martha, reach in my saddle bag and bring out that knife."

Martha went over to his horse and brought back a knife. She held it up.

"Is that yours?" Mersey asked.

Tim nodded, feeling his throat tighten a little.

"That's all I wanted to know," Mersey said. "That's the knife found in Borden's throat. Shelley saw it, I saw it, two clerks from the hardware store saw it and Doc Masters saw it."

"When?" Tim asked.

"When we came back for the body."

"That wasn't the agate-handled knife in Borden's throat when I saw him!" Tim said in a thick voice. "You damn jugheaded fool! While you were downstairs gettin' the men to take Borden away, somebody switched the knives on you!"

"With the door locked? Don't make me laugh."

"The window was open."

"It was not. I locked it."

"Then somebody got the key."

"They did not. I had it in my pocket."

"Then they got Shelley's passkey."

"They did not. It was in his pocket. He went with me."

Tim looked at Martha, and her eyes held his glance for ten long seconds. "I didn't kill Borden," Tim said quietly, stubbornly.

Mersey laughed shortly. "You'll get a chance to tell that to twelve jaspers, who don't believe in fairy tales, mister. Stand up."

Tim came erect, his lips grim.

"Jeff, help me get him on his horse," Mersey said.

"Hell with you," Jeff replied with mountainous calm.

"You got to," Mersey said. "I'm the law and I command you to help me get him on his horse. If you don't get him on and tie him in his saddle, you're liable to arrest!"

"Hell with you," Jeff repeated.

Mersey's face was getting red. He couldn't turn his attention to Jeff for fear Tim would make a break. He said in a choked voice, "Martha, I guess you got to do it."

Martha backed away. "What Jeff said goes for me, too," she answered quietly.

Tim felt a quiet exultation within him. She didn't believe him a murderer. Neither did Jeff. He said, "You figure my word is any good, Mersey?"

Mersey didn't answer for a moment, then said, "Not much."

Tim flushed. "Well, you've got it for what it's worth. I'll get on my horse and won't make a break. You can tie me in the saddle if you want."

Mersey hesitated. Finally he said, "I guess I got to. Only remember this, mister. There's only one thing I'd rather do than put a slug in your back, and that's put two of them there. Now get your horse."

Two hours later Tim was in the Morgan County jail. It was a good jail, built of stone, containing six cells of which his was the first on the left as you went into the cell block, and it was as escape-proof as death. A little less than twenty-four hours after he had arrived here to help the law of Morgan County, that same law had him in jail. And on a very convincing murder charge.

4

Where the Tornado River left the foothills, it flowed west into Tornado Basin; it was both wide and swift, fed by the snows of the peaks. Jeff Hardy, when the first settler came into the valley, got help to build a bridge. That bridge had been rebuilt four times, until now it was of solid planking, roomy, with its piles deep driven into the river bed and shored with rock.

On this night Ben Wiley, with two of his fellow nesters,

lounged around a fire beneath it. They were guards of a sort, for if Sands was to cross safely any big body of sheep it must be by this bridge. The fourth guard, McCoy by name, was on top.

All four of them had seen a herd of Sands' sheep bedded down on the opposite bank that evening. Wiley, as was his way, was brooding on it like an undecided man is apt to do when he sees potential trouble in the offing. He was thinking of the loose agreement among the nesters which had been to take the bridge watch turn about. If trouble was coming it would be useless for him to fight, and Wiley, a practical man, was wondering how to profit by his strange position.

He prodded the fire, squatting on his haunches, and regarded his two ragged mates.

"How many shells we got?" he asked suddenly.

"Twenty—twenty-five," one of the nesters answered.

Wiley grinned thinly, his beard-stubbled face creasing in two long lines.

"That gonna be enough for you two if he decides to cross?"

"Two? There's four of us here, ain't there?"

"McCoy ain't having any," Wiley said. "Neither am I."

It was the old argument he was hammering home and had been ever since the meeting. This time, however, he was spared further talk. McCoy leaned his head over the bridge rail and called, "Ben, someone's coming."

Like a scuttling rabbit, Wiley grabbed a rifle and dodged up the bank. One of the nesters observed to the other, "Looks like he wants a runnin' head start if anything breaks."

"Can't say as I blame him," the other growled.

On the top of the bridge, Wiley joined McCoy. Together they could make out the sound of a man approaching. Soon his shape bulked dark in the night ahead of them and he stopped.

"Wiley," he called.

"Yeah?"

The man came closer. "Boss wants to see you."

"Sands you mean?" Wiley said.

"That's right. He's in camp."

Wiley hesitated only a moment. Like all troublesome men, he realized that he had a nuisance value, and he had already been shrewd enough to point that out to any of Sands' men who would listen. He handed his rifle to McCoy and fell in beside the messenger. They walked back over the bridge. Once Wiley said, "I only got one thing against your damn sheep, and that's their stink." His companion laughed.

"Me, too. I just came off a horse-wrangling job, but for a hundred and fifty a month I'll take sheep, stink and all."

The road turned sharp right at the end of the bridge. The two horses were waiting in the brush by it, faintly visible in the low moon. They mounted and the sheep guard struck off toward the south. Soon they saw a fire but they skirted this, still heading south. Presently, where the land tilted to the river bluff and plains beyond, they saw another fire. It was the second sheep camp. A brush wickiup had been built by the Mexican sheepherder who was now rustling more wood for the fire. Sands, squatted at the mouth of the wickiup, was warming his hands. He looked up at Wiley's approach but did not speak, and Wiley's spirits rose at sight of him. This meant business.

Wiley shuffled up to the fire, casting around for more men. Sands observing him, said, cool contempt in his voice, "If you think this is a trap, you're welcome to ride off."

Wiley said, "Trap for what? I ain't worth it."

"You nesters are used to eating humble pie, I take it."

"Sometimes," Wiley said.

"Sit down."

Wiley squatted across the fire and rolled a smoke from his sack of dust. Sands watched him, his black eyes contemptuous, calculating.

"Tell me," he said suddenly, "what would you do if I sent ten men across that bridge tonight?"

"Run," Wiley said briefly and truthfully.

Sands smiled. "What about the others?"

"They'd get shot, maybe."

"They know that, do they?"

"I been trying to tell 'em for three days."

Sands nodded. "At least you know self-preservation when you see it." He added after a pause, "How much would it cost me to make them see it, too?"

Wiley said shrewdly, "How good do you want them to see it?"

"So well," Sands said, "that they'll pick up and leave."

"Their places, you mean?"

"Of course."

Wiley scoured his chin thoughtfully, staring into the fire. "McCoy would see it for three thousand dollars," he said. "So would I. Them others might not see it at all at first, but they'd sure as hell get cold and go home tonight for a couple hundred each."

Sands said, "And stay home?"

Wiley laughed. "Mister, they'll all stay home. Nobody likes gunmen when they ride in gangs of a dozen or so."

Sands stroked his saber mustaches thoughtfully. "Are those your sentiments alone?"

"I tell you they won't fight. They can't. Martha Kincaid has been trying to work 'em up for two months now. They had their own sheriff behind 'em and they was a dozen strong, but a good half of 'em figure they'd just as soon give up their places without a scrap so's they can sit by and watch them big cattlemen get hell whipped out of 'em. I figure that way, too."

"But you want money," Sands said.

Wiley nodded. "That's right. And it's worth it to you. I'll tell you why. If I can't raise three thousand dollars' worth of hell on my own hook by shooting your herders, stealing your supplies, taking pot shots at your camp, poisoning your water holes, then I'm wide of my guess. What do you think?"

"I think so, too," Sands agreed. "Do the others think that?"

Wiley spat. "Nope. I'm just cussed."

Sands stared into the fire a long moment, then he rose, walked into the wickiup and returned with a heavy canvas sack. Before Wiley's greedy eyes he counted out three thousand dollars in gold coins. He said suddenly, "How much land have you?"

"Half section," Wiley replied.

"You're a liar," Sands said calmly. "You've got a homestead, a hundred and sixty acres. I made sure of that in Morgan Tanks."

Wiley grinned sheepishly. "That's right. I just wanted you to figure you're getting your money's worth."

From his inner coat pocket Sands pulled out a thick sheaf of papers, from which he took a single sheet and handed it to Wiley. It was a warranty deed which automatically blanketed everything that Wiley owned.

"Sign it," Sands said. A whistle from him brought two men from out of the night. The deed was signed and witnessed.

When Wiley had the money he said, "About them others, you want me to take their money to them?"

"Don't be a fool," Sands said. "We've got two hours to wait till dawn. I'll go with you then, and take care of them. Make yourself comfortable." He smiled meagerly. "If I gave that money to you, you'd be half way up the Tornado Peaks with it by sunup."

He turned to his men and gave them instructions. They were to inform the herders of the five bands nearest the bridge to be ready to move at dawn. Wiley was forgotten. Sands moved in and out of camp without noticing him.

When false dawn began to gray the east, Sands said, "Come along." This time they rode across the bridge. McCoy came with them as they went below to the fire. Erickson and Worth were both asleep, their backs turned to the coals.

Wiley wakened them and stoked the fire. Worth was the first to speak. "What's he doing here?" he asked Wiley, indicating Sands.

Wiley pulled out a handful of gold coins and jingled them. "Him? He's Santa Claus. You'd better listen." His face was flushed with success.

Sands spoke curtly. "Will either of you sell out your holdings to me? For three thousand each?"

Worth and Erickson declined with profanity.

Sands smiled narrowly. "I'm afraid I'm through asking," he said. "From now on I'm telling you. I want you to clear out from this bridge—now."

"What if we don't?" Worth said.

"I'm crossing five thousand sheep in about ten minutes. I'd prefer they weren't stampeded by the smell of fresh blood."

Erickson said, "You talk mighty damn big for a man that's alone among four of us with guns."

"Alone?" Sands echoed ironically. "There must be a dozen of my men on the bridge above us by now."

Wiley laughed softly, pleased with himself. Sands counted out several gold coins into two piles in front of the fire and indicated them with a tired gesture. "I always pay for what I take. This is for leaving—now. Good by, gentlemen."

At that moment the drumming of myriad sheep hooves was carried across the bridge planking. Worth and Erickson, poor men both, sullenly took the money and disappeared into the dawn.

While five thousand sheep made talking under the bridge almost impossible, McCoy signed away his claim on the Tornado Basin. By full sunup, Sands had his toe hold, as legal as any other, and the blatting of loose-herded sheep stirred the surprised birds of the river bottom in their morning song.

5

For a range-bred man, nine o'clock was not the time for breakfast, but Will Mersey had lost too much sleep over this prisoner to want to pamper him. Will ate at nine and so did Tim—as an afterthought of Will's.

At nine-thirty Will Mersey, at peace with the world for the first time in some days, entered his office behind four inches of cigar to find Julie Sands waiting there. She was wearing a light summer dress trimmed with bands of maroon silk and she was bareheaded. Will Mersey yanked off his hat at sight of her, his face reflecting honest puzzlement.

"Am I allowed to visit your prisoner?" she asked.

"If you can stand the sight of a murderer I reckon you are, Miss Sands," Will replied. It went against his grain to be polite to a sheepman's daughter, but this was something extra-special in the way of daughters, Will admitted to himself. He even managed the semblance of a smile.

"I don't think that's proven yet, is it?" Julie said.

"Maybe you better ask him," Will murmured. From his pocket he drew out two heavy keys, and with the first unlocked the corridor door. With the second he unlocked the cell door and Julie entered.

Tim was sitting on the cot whose blankets were already made up. His breakfast tray was on the floor. Surprise showed in his lean face at sight of the girl, but he said nothing until Will Mersey had left.

Then he said, "I didn't reckon I'd ever get a chance to thank you, miss, for saving my neck that night." He smiled fleetingly and indicated the cot, and Julie sat down on it. He regarded her in a puzzled manner. "Maybe nobody's told you who I am."

"A range detective, aren't you?" Julie asked. "Sent here to drive out my father?"

Tim nodded. "I just didn't want to mislead you, or get you in trouble."

"Trouble like what?"

"Well, if I ever get out of here I'll fight your father until one of us goes down. Maybe he wouldn't like your seeing me." He said it gravely, without smiling.

Julie said coldly, "Dad and I go our own ways and mostly they are opposite. Maybe you gathered that from the other night."

Tim grinned now. "Sort of." He rather liked the way this girl talked.

"But I like to be fair," Julie went on. "I think he's ruthless and is headed for real trouble, but I don't think he's lost to all honor."

Tim said nothing, only watched her troubled and grave face.

"You do, don't you?" she said.

"He saved me from a jam," Tim said evasively.

"And got you in a worse one."

"That fight. Oh, that——"

"No, this. You think he's the cause of your being here, don't you? You think he searched your room for your knife and substituted it."

Tim felt the color crawl into his face. "I don't know," he said honestly. "If I didn't knock him out for more than a few minutes I reckon he could have planted the knife. If he was out for half an hour then he couldn't have done it."

"He was unconscious for an hour," Julie said earnestly. "I was with him all that time. I was putting cold towels on his head when the deputy came up with the others to get the body. I know he didn't do it. I know his men didn't do it. Not," she added bitterly, "that his men wouldn't do it."

Or Sands either, Tim thought grimly, remembering Sands' intention of having Borden killed. But he said nothing, only scowled faintly.

"You don't believe me?" Julie said.

"Of course I do," Tim said quickly. "But by believing you, I reckon I've got to believe in something else that don't seem possible."

"What?"

Tim sat down beside her. "Look, Miss Julie, when Mersey arrested me yesterday he said that he locked both the door and the window of the room that held Borden's body. He and Shelley, the clerk, had both the key and the passkey on them. When that door was locked the knife in Borden's throat was not mine. I know. I saw it. It was an agate-handled knife. When the door was unlocked my knife had been substituted. Who got in? How? Why?"

Julie thought a moment. "Was your room like mine?" she asked.

Tim remembered both and nodded.

"Then the murderer must have been in the room all the time."

"Where?"

"In the wardrobe."

Tim stared at her. "Could it—— Sure, a man could hide in it! But how did he get my knife?"

Julie said irrelevantly. "You changed rooms, didn't you? Dad said you did."

"Yes."

"Then after Dad and you left the deputy and he locked the door, couldn't the man in the wardrobe slip into your room through the window, get your knife, come back, exchange it and leave?"

"But the window was still locked when Mersey came back," Tim said.

"He hid again in the wardrobe. They didn't find him the first time. Why should they the second? Then he could have slipped out after they had taken Borden's body away."

Tim nodded slowly, his forehead creased with a scowl.

"You don't want to believe it, do you?" Julie said.

Tim looked guiltily at her. "Not much," he said. "I like to

know who I'm fighting. I've been fighting Sands up to now, with a lot of narrow-gauge jugheads to hinder me. Now it looks like I'm fighting somebody else."

"Make no mistake," Julie said. "You're still fighting Father. He hates you."

"Why shouldn't he? I'm a cowman."

"It isn't that," Julie replied. "We were cow folks once. Dad just looks on cowmen as fools. Cowmen raise cows for money. Sheepmen raise sheep for money. There's more money in sheep, therefore, all cowmen should be sheepmen. Or if they aren't they should at least allow a sheepman the right to live. They don't. Dad started out to fight that. He's fought and won so long that it's a mania with him now. He doesn't need money, clothes, good food, any of the luxuries money will buy. All he needs is to win. That's what he lives for."

She laughed shortly, bitterly. "Give him the sight of a peaceful, prosperous cattle range and he is not content until he sees it overrun with sheep."

"He's a hard man," Tim agreed.

"So hard he killed my mother," Julie said tonelessly. "So hard that he will drive me away from him."

"Why do you stay?" Tim asked curiously.

"Hope," Julie said curtly. "I can remember when I was a little girl. He liked friends—and had them. He was curious about everything. He loved life. I keep hoping when this mania runs its course that he'll be like that again. And I owe him good times. This hasn't been easy even on him."

"But he won't win this time," Tim said quietly.

Julie looked at him searchingly. "That's what I'm afraid of. You see, I believe you're the kind of a man who always wins, too."

"Not always."

"But often enough that your face shows it," Julie murmured, a trace of bitterness in her voice. "I can tell. Success marks a man. It gives him a different look, makes him hard and willing to trample on people." She smiled faintly. "It's losing once in a while that makes people human."

Tim said gently, "You're pretty young to have learned that, Julie."

"I've had to. And I can tell it to you because I think you understand. You see, Dad was a lot like you when he was young, people say. He was prideful and bullheaded, and when his temper broke, people were afraid of him—like they are of you."

She rose and smoothed out her dress, and Tim rose with her, listening to her embarrassed little laugh. "It's funny," she said. "I didn't mean to say this when I came in here. I only wanted to tell you that Dad was innocent of framing this murder charge against you."

"I believe you," Tim said. "That's—well, I'll never hold that against him."

"But down in your heart you aren't sure," Julie said quietly. "Isn't that it?"

Tim grinned and nodded without saying anything.

"Then I'll show you," Julie said wearily. "I don't know who murdered Borden, but I'm going to try and find out. And if it turns out to be Dad I won't hide it from you. I'll tell the truth."

At that moment the corridor door swung open, and Will Mersey hurried into the cell block. "You'll have to leave now, Miss Sands," he said abruptly.

"What—have I done anything wrong?" Julie asked coldly.

Will Mersey smiled grimly. "Not you. It's your old man, miss. He's moved across the Tornado with five thousand sheep. I got to get out there before all hell busts loose."

Tim heard Julie sigh before she started out. She smiled fleetingly at Tim as the cell door was locked after her. Out in the office she smiled again at a huge old man who doffed his hat to her in stately courtliness. Outside, she turned toward the hotel, and had not taken a dozen steps before she was aware someone was following her.

She stopped and turned and spoke to a slight, still-faced puncher who had dropped in five paces behind her.

"As long as Dad's going to have you watch me," she said in a cold, imperious voice, "there's no use in the two of us looking like an Indian and his squaw. Walk up here with me, St. Cloud, and please don't talk."

Jeff Hardy had brought the news to Mersey, after Martha Kincaid brought it to him. He stood there in the office, a hulking, quiet man, while Will Mersey ushered Julie out, then watched Will make a grab for a gun at the wall rack.

Will shooed him out of the office, locked it, and set off at a swift pace downstreet for the livery stable.

"Wait a minute," Jeff said, now beside him. "What about your prisoner? You may not be back for a coupla days."

"Let him starve!" Mersey said bitterly. "If it hadn't been for him this never would have happened!"

"Go saddle your horse," Jeff said. "I'll meet you at the stable."

He stopped at the Oriental Café and there arranged to have three meals a day poked through the bars to Tim Enever until Will's return. Afterward he joined Will, and they rode out of town toward the southeast in the direction of the bridge. Jeff, out of curiosity, wanted to stay with Will Mersey to see what he would do. He also wanted to see Warner Sands and get some idea of the man, and this seemed to be his chance. There was another idea in the back of Jeff's mind, too. It was put there by the look of hopelessness on Martha Kincaid's face this morning when she brought him the news. Martha had quit fighting. Sands had made the crucial move while the only man who could help Martha fight him was in jail. Jeff didn't blame her for feeling the way she did, only he decided it wasn't healthy and that something would have to be done about it. When he observed Will Mersey stuff the keys to both the corridor door and the cell block in his pocket as they left the jail, he decided Will was the logical man to stick with.

They found the sheep, as reported, clustered to the north

of the bridge on the land claimed by McCoy and Wiley. Those two, however, were not around. Two riders stopped them by the bridge and wanted to know their business. They were a tough-looking pair with carbines in their saddle boots and a gun on each hip.

"You got any business around here?" one of them asked Mersey.

Mersey's temper had been simmering during the whole ride. Now he leaned over his saddle horn and said, "Mister, I was born and raised in this country. I happen to work here. If you ask me that again, so help me, I'll break you into so many pieces they can serve you for a wet hash."

"You're trespassin'," the rider growled.

"I don't give a damn if I'm growin' flowers. Get out of my way!"

It was the other rider who recognized Mersey. He nudged his companion to silence and Mersey and Jeff passed. Already they were passing stray bands of grazing sheep which were strung along the low river bluff.

Sands, apparently, had taken over Wiley's shack as his headquarters. A half-dozen ponies were tethered at the door, and smoke issued from the chimney. A guard posted at the door saw them and disappeared inside, and by the time they approached the place, Sands was standing in the dooryard of the main shack. He looked a little tired and pale this morning.

Mersey pulled up and folded his arms on the saddle horn. His tone was a little more respectful now, but there was iron in it, Jeff noticed.

"You don't believe what people tell you, do you, Sands?"

"Sometimes, why?"

"I thought I told you to stay on that side of the river with your woollies."

"You did. But there's a law in this country that says a man is entitled to do anything—or almost anything—on his own property."

"This yours?"

"It is. Since this morning."

Mersey's jaw clamped shut with a click. "Wiley sold out to you, eh?"

"McCoy, too."

"That gives you a half section, don't it?"

"Roughly."

"Then you better stay on it."

"Did Wiley stay on it?" Sands asked softly.

"He had cows."

"Ah." Sands smiled and looked over at Jeff Hardy, who was regarding him with a perfectly impassive face from his big horse. "There's a difference, eh? Well, gentlemen, there is no difference to me. The fashion in this country is to homestead a place where there's water and build your house on it. After that, you take as much of the surrounding range as you can hold." His eyes narrowed a little. "I think I can hold a little more than a half section, Mersey. At least I always have so far."

"The minute you move out onto that free grass there'll be a fight, and the minute there's a fight I'll have a warrant out for you as the man who started it. And I'll get you, too, Sands," Mersey said grimly.

"That remains to be seen," Sands said impudently. "I know my rights as well as the next man. As for your coming to get me when the fight starts, Mersey, you'd better come smoking."

"I will."

"Then good day."

Once out of sight of the cabin Jeff Hardy asked placidly, "Well? What next, Will?"

"If he's goin' to move onto this grass soon then it'll be Proctor's grass he's on. I'm goin' up and talk to Proctor. You comin'?" Will was in a savage temper, and the memory of Sands' words seemed to feed it.

"I am not," Jeff said mildly. "You won't get Proctor to fight. There's him and seven hands against Sands and his gunnies. He'll fash around and kill a few sheep and get his place burned down for it, that's all."

"Well, I aim to see him anyway."

"When'll you get all your business done, Will?"

"Not before midafternoon, I reckon."

"Goin' back to town then?"

"Might's well."

"Stop in for me. I'm goin', too," Jeff said.

They parted and Jeff rode on north toward the Ox-Bow. It was a perfect summer day with the ground breeze ruffling the buffalo grass, and Jeff regarded the country with a homely pleasure. The calf crop had been good here in sheltered Tornado Basin, and as he rode on through scattered herds, he saw them frisking about with their mothers, clean as the grass they ate. He could remember seeing antelope playing that way the first year he came here. That was a long time ago when the country was good. It was still good, he reflected, but it didn't seem as if it was going to stay that way for long. It put him in mind of something he had thought of this morning, and he thought more about it, giving his horse its head.

When he rode into the corral lot before noon, the Ox-Bow looked deserted. Jeff put up his horse and ambled into the house, going in by the kitchen way. Charlie, the Chinese cook, had some food laid out ready for him. He was lazily watching an ovenful of bread, and had been practicing on his concertina up till now. He put the concertina away when Jeff came in, since it was a tacit agreement between them that the only practice hours allowed were those when Jeff was away.

Jeff sat down to his meal, pouring out his coffee first and slugging down two cups as an appetizer.

"Charlie, you remember the vegetable cellar up at the old house that burned down?" he asked presently.

"Sure."

"You been up there lately?"

"Catchum walk there last Sunday," Charlie said.

"That cellar caved in yet?"

Charlie stopped to consider. The old place, a log affair, had been built a mile or so from the present ranch on an eminence of the foothills. It had long since served its purpose, which was a fort against the Indians, and Jeff had been glad when it burned and he could build this place. That was fifteen years ago. It was a nice walk up there, and Charlie usually took it when he could find a few spare hours away from the kitchen and the bull cook, who cooked for the hands.

"Still there. Some damfool ride through it some night, alla horseback and bleak leg."

"You're sure the roof ain't caved?"

"Sure. Sure."

Jeff grunted and went on eating. Afterward, he rode up to the old site and took a look at the cellar himself. It was walled with field stone and roofed with sturdy logs upon which dirt had been piled to catch seed grass. Now, the roof was sod. Jeff stepped down inside. It was darker than the depths of a well, but cool and certainly dry. The tight door had kept out snakes and mice, and it had the musty smell of a place that needed airing. Jeff grunted. "Ought to do," he murmured. "Ain't a hotel, but nobody'd think of lookin' here."

He returned to the house and barely had time to snatch a nap before Will Mersey rode into the place. Jeff, who usually cursed at any interruption of his siesta, joined Will with unaccustomed alacrity and the best of spirits.

Will was still in a foul mood. True to Jeff's prediction, Proctor had sworn that he'd have the scalp of Sands if so much as one damn sheep poked his face onto Circle P grass. Furthermore, he didn't want the help of the sheriff's office or anyone else. When he got so feeble he couldn't fight his own fights, then he'd call for help and not before.

Jeff didn't laugh. "Give your horse a drink while I saddle up."

When he returned from the corral he had a new saddle on

his big buckskin. Mersey, looking at it, said, "You goin' out prowlin'?"

"Prowlin'?"

"Why the blankets then?"

Jeff looked down at them and laughed. "Damn if I saw 'em. My other saddle was wet, so I changed." But he did not take the blankets off. "Sure you won't stay for supper?" he asked of Will, just as they were ready to leave.

Will said, "Well, I ain't been asked."

"Look here, did you get a feed at Proctor's?"

"Nope."

"Then you better light and have a bite."

"You ain't in a hurry?"

"Shucks, that can wait. I'll have Charlie rustle you somethin'."

Dismounting again, Jeff grinned secretly. It had worked out to perfection. He had delayed their start an hour, which would put the last half of their journey in darkness, and still had not made Will suspicious.

An hour later they set out for Morgan Tanks. Sunset and darkness found them still on the road, discussing the possibilities of the coming fight. They were riding into the valley of Wagon Tongue Creek, a feeder to the Tornado. It was a deep creek, perhaps twenty-five feet wide, and they would cross it where the road dipped down to a ford. Few people besides Jeff knew that the ford had once been a beaver dam, and that just a few feet down stream from it, it dropped off into a pool, and a deep one. Before the beavers had been trapped out and their dam smashed by the wagon road, Jeff used the place for a swimming hole.

He kept tickling his horse's withers as they loped down toward the creek, and the big chestnut started to shy in protest.

"What's eatin' him?" Will asked.

"Something's spookin' him down here. A skunk, maybe," Jeff said idly.

The chestnut's antics forced Will to pull his horse over to

the left, a little off the road, and this was the way they
entered the stream. They no sooner hit the water than Jeff
pulled his chestnut over and reared him. Will pulled his
horse over, too, to get out of the way, and then it happened.

Will's horse lost its footing suddenly, pawed the stream
bed, and then slipped sideways. Will sloped out of the saddle
into the water to avoid being pinned under, and immediately
found that he was in swimming water. His horse discovered
it also, and swam to the bank and climbed out, Will hanging
onto his tail. Jeff was waiting, his face grave.

"Well, don't that beat hell," Jeff said, helping Will out.
"He slip?"

"No, there's a bank there," Will sputtered. "It's deep,
over my head."

Jeff caught Will's horse and then looked at his companion. "Will, you're a sorry sight," he observed. "You can't
ride to town in wet clothes."

Will's teeth were chattering by now. "I'll wring 'em out
and make a run for it."

"You'll do nothin' of the kind," Jeff put in. "You'll catch
pnewmony sure as shooting." He suddenly snapped his fingers. "Why, hell! I knew them blankets would come in
handy. Look, you shuck off them clothes, Will, and I'll build
up a fire. You hunker down in these blankets till I dry your
clothes. It won't take a half-hour."

To a man in Will Mersey's condition this was a welcome
suggestion. He stripped and crawled into Jeff's blankets,
while Jeff built up a roaring fire on the creek bank.

Jeff was very careful not to say much. He wanted nature
to take its course. And, just as he had figured, when Will
quit shivering and got warm he started to drowse. Jeff squatted on his heels away from the blazing fire and kept one eye
on Will's steaming clothes, the other on Will. Within ten
minutes Will was asleep.

Jeff moved unconcernedly to the fire, felt of Will's pants,
deemed them dry, took them off the stick, folded them and
stole a glance at Will. He was sleeping.

Jeff stole quietly out of the firelight. Once there, he fumbled around in the pockets and finally brought forth the two jail keys, which were wedged crosswise in a hip pocket. Then he started his search. He found a nice-sized pine tree and hunted its trunk, then went to the next. Soon he had gathered a handful of pine pitch. This he took to the fire, laid on a stone and watched it melt together. After it had cooled somewhat he worked it out into a flat cake, and, with an eye on the sleeping deputy, took very accurate impressions of the two keys. Once he was finished he returned the keys to Will's pants, took the pitch down to the stream bank, plunged it in cold water to harden it, then dug out some wet moss from the bank, wrapped the pitch carefully in it, and placed it in the breast pocket of his shirt where it was open to the cool night breeze.

When Will's clothes were dry Jeff wakened him and they rode the seven-odd miles into Morgan Tanks, parting at the hotel. Jeff got a drink at the Gem saloon across from the livery stable, then sauntered down the deserted main street to the four corners and turned up the cross street.

At McBane's blacksmith shop a shaft of light thrown out into the dust of the street showed that Jim McBane was still working. He was a small man with the grime of ten years of forging scoured into his face. A freighter, passing through south, had broken a felly in the mountain pass, and McBane had a wheelwright job that would keep him open for several hours.

"Lemme fiddle around then?" Jeff asked. "I got somethin' to fix."

"Go ahead," McBane said. "Only keep out of my way."

Jeff went to the workbench. There, without McBane seeing or caring what he was doing, he made two rough keys and filed them into the shapes required to fit the pitch mold. That finished, he threw the pitch in the fire, thanked McBane and sauntered off into the night. He took a trial walk down the main street to see if there was a light in the sheriff's office or the jail behind it. There was not. He circled

around and came back by way of the alley. The window at
the end of the jail was high up in the wall, so that he had to
drag a barrel from behind the Gem saloon and stand on it to
put his face even with the sill.

"Tim!" he called. He got no answer and tried again. This
time he got a sleepy reply.

"Yeah?"

"Git awake, boy."

"All right," Tim said. His voice was crisper, holding a
little excitement.

"You got a match?"

"Sure."

"Light it."

Tim did. By its light Jeff could see that Tim was at the
end of the corridor in the first cell, the farthest from him. He
poked his big fist between the bars and followed it with his
arm. Then he tossed the keys on the floor and they came to
a skidding stop in front of Tim's cell.

"Come on out," Jeff said. "Walk right out. I'll wait for
you on the hotel porch."

He went around to the street and found a chair on the
deserted hotel porch. In less than five minutes the door to
the sheriff's office opened casually and Tim Enever stepped
out. He looked up and down the street, crossed to the porch
and took a chair by Jeff.

Jeff looked at Tim. "Well, what do you aim to do now?
High tail it out of the country before they catch you?"

"I'm stickin'," Tim said quietly. "I want a shave first and
a gun second and a place to hide third."

"I'd get out if I was you," Jeff insisted.

"You would like hell!" Tim growled. "Neither am I."

Jeff chuckled and recrossed his legs. "Well, son, you want
advice?"

"I do."

"You might's well be hung for a horse thief as a murderer.
First thing I'd do would be to steal a horse. That black in
front of the Gem looks like a stayer. Ride out to my place,

get a shave, get a meal and take the gun Charlie gives you. Then go with him to the place you'll hide out. I'll be in sometime tomorrow and see you. I just want to stick around and see how Mersey takes it."

"But Martha Kincaid will——"

"Martha be damned!" Jeff said roughly. "One thing at a time. If she didn't need you did you s'pose I'd of got you out? And if she can't wait don't you suppose I'd tell you?"

He watched Tim ride calmly out of town on a stolen horse, then got up, went inside, got a room and went up to bed, content.

6

Tim arrived at the Ox-Bow in the small hours of the morning. True to what Jeff had said, Charlie, who slept on a cot in the lean-to off the kitchen, was waiting for him. Tim was out of the mood for his shave now, and Charlie, after giving him a carbine, some ammunition, two guns, a belt of shells and a sack of food, led the way through the night up the ridge and over to the old house foundation and its cellar.

Tim beheld his new home with complete distaste, and did not even bother to examine it by the light of Charlie's lantern. When the cook left him Tim let the night settle down about him. It did not bring him any rest. Far off in the hills he could hear two coyotes barking. Down in the Basin the long howl of a ranch dog drifted up to him. But the night held no peace for him, and the thought of turning into blankets now was intolerable. Off to the south Sands would wake to a new day, a day in which he would push his sheep a little further into the Basin while he, Tim, slept. And there was Martha Kincaid. Had she given up?

Tim looked at the stars and made a sudden decision. Dawn was not far off. By daylight he could be with her, learning the news, plotting out the next almost hopeless move against Sands.

He took his rifle and left the ridge, headed for the ranch. It lay silent under the stars, and he made his way to the corral. The dozen horses there spooked at his approach. Tim singled out the black to which he had helped himself in Morgan Tanks, cut him out and saddled him again. Once headed for Martha Kincaid's, he felt easier in his mind. At least this was not sitting in jail, nor was it exchanging that jail for a hiding place in a deserted vegetable cellar.

Sunup found him well on his way to the Tornado bluffs. He left the road at daylight and kept to whatever cover he could find.

It was almost seven o'clock, he figured, when he came to the road that led to Martha Kincaid's. He was hungry, a little tired from his night's ride, and the thought of seeing her again made him impatiently touch the black in the flanks. In another minute he would round the clay dunes and be in sight of her place. Already he could see the smoke from her breakfast fire lifting into the morning sky.

When he got to the dunes and in sight of the house, he stopped suddenly and pulled his horse out of sight. Martha was standing in the yard talking to a strange man on horseback. Tim watched the conversation with growing unease. Was it somebody from town who already had thought of searching her place for him?

And even while he was watching, it happened. The man leaned over in the saddle, put an arm around Martha's waist and hauled her up and across the saddle. He pulled his horse into a rear, wheeled, and then started off toward the river, Martha struggling frantically to free herself.

Tim's first impulse was to put spurs to his black and take off in pursuit. But whoever it was, when he learned he was being followed, would probably drop Martha or else, using her as a shield, make his getaway.

Tim whipped out his carbine as he slid out of the saddle and bellied down in the clay. The rider appeared to be in no hurry, and his broad back was to Tim. For one brief instant Tim's courage deserted him. If he should go wide of his mark he might hit her. Then, his fears were dissolved, for the man hoisted Martha to a sitting position in front of him.

Tim held his breath and lined his sights carefully until the horse's rump was in the groove of the two sights. Then he lifted and brought the barrel down again. There in the groove, was the man's Stetson, his head and now his neck. Tim squeezed the trigger, and without waiting to see what had happened he swung up into the saddle. It was long range; he could only hope the gun was accurate.

When he looked again it was just in time to see the man slope sideways out of the saddle. Martha jumped clear, and to the left. The rider pitched loosely out of the saddle, hit the ground, and then his horse, alarmed, began to run. The rider's right foot had slipped through the stirrup and the horse was dragging him.

Tim put spurs to his black and raced past the house and down the slope to Martha. She was watching the stampeded horse with a kind of breathless horror on her face.

When she whirled to face Tim amazement displaced that horror. "Tim! Was it you who shot?"

"Are you all right?" Tim asked huskily.

"Yes, only—look!" She pointed to the galloping horse, dragging its gruesome burden down the flinty boulder-strewn slope to the bottom lands. "You've got to catch him, Tim! It's—it's awful!"

Tim set out after the stampeded bay horse, but his black was tired. He thought to cut off the horse which was making a slow half circle to the east, but when the frantic bay caught sight of him, he changed his direction. Now Tim gained rapidly on him. Suddenly, the bay stopped and started to plunge and kick, trying to rid himself of the terrifying burden he was dragging. Tim rode up and stepped out of the saddle, shaking out his rope. The bay was quieting.

Tim made a quick cast, and the loop settled around the bay's neck. Now, instead of stampeding again, the bay stood still, trembling with fright, but glad of human help. Slowly, hand over hand on the taut rope, Tim approached him, talking soothingly. The bay made no move, but his eyes were wicked with fright, and the smell of blood was in his nostrils.

When Tim had quieted him he uncinched the saddle and led the bay out from under it and away from the man on the ground. Once the horse was calm, Tim came back to look at the man.

At first glance what was recognizable of him looked to be Will Mersey. The face was a battered pulp where it had been dragged over the flinty slope, but the man's hair was the mottled piebald color of Will Mersey's and their builds were similar. The clothes, however, were not the deputy's. Strangely enough, the man was wearing fancy, hand-stitched boots. His guns, instead of Will Mersey's cedar-handled Colts, probably would have been pearl handled to fit the tooled-leather silver-mounted cartridge belt. Tim felt a little sick as he turned away from the man. His shot had done the work, so that the rider had not suffered through the dragging. The slug had taken him between the shoulders and broken his back.

Tim mounted and led the bay back up the slope to the shack, his face thoughtful.

Martha was sitting on the doorstep, still trembling in spite of the warming morning sun.

"What happened?" Tim wanted to know.

"I—I don't know," Martha stammered weakly. "It's one of Sands' gunmen, I think. He stopped by and asked if I would give him breakfast. I said I would, even if he was a sheepman. He watched me all through breakfast until I began to get uncomfortable. He tried to kiss me, Tim. I slapped his face. Then he got his horse and called me out of the house. I guess you saw the rest." She looked up at Tim and smiled weakly. "I'm not going to cry—only I was scared."

"Look here," Tim said earnestly. "You've got to move over to Jeff's. It isn't safe here."

"Don't talk for a minute, Tim," Martha said. "Don't look at me."

Tim smiled and looked away. When he turned back Martha had control of herself. A little of the color was back in her face as she stood up and smiled at Tim. "But what are you doing here?"

"Jeff broke me out of jail."

Martha laughed shakily, and a look of worry crept into her eyes. "But won't they be after you?"

"Mersey will, I reckon."

"But not before you have time to eat breakfast."

"No."

They went inside. While Martha got him breakfast she told him of what had happened while he was gone. Wiley, McCoy, Worth and Erickson had all sold out now. That left nine stubborn nesters, but they were fast weakening. When they sold out that left only seven big ranchers, with their crews, between Sands and all of the Tornado Basin that he wanted to take.

"They don't see it yet?" Tim asked quietly.

"They're further from it than ever!" Martha said bitterly, hopelessly. "It looks like we're licked, Tim. They can still band together and drive him out if every rancher and his crew and every nester throw together. But we can't make them! It's impossible!"

Tim said nothing, and Martha went on. "If you were free to help, Tim, it might be different. But you'll have to hide now. Mersey will hunt you down, or try to, in between threats to Sands. And Jeff and I can't do it alone. He's too old, Tim, and I'm a woman."

"Yeah, Mersey," Tim murmured. "With that jug-headed ranahan out of the way I could help you. The others don't care. It's just Mersey, with his damn bullheadedness!"

"But he isn't out of the way!" Martha cried. "You'll have to hide out in the hills, Tim, and watch it all happen from there."

Tim was scowling at his plate, his eyes dreamy. Martha was about to speak again when she noticed it. Slowly, Tim laid down his fork, and his beard-stubbled face was puzzled as he looked up at her.

"What is it, Tim?"

"Somethin' I just thought of," Tim answered slowly. "Maybe it's somethin' that will get Will Mersey out of the way and band these Tornado Basin cattlemen together all in one move."

"What?"

Tim pushed back his chair and rubbed his cheek with the flat of his hand, then looked up at Martha. "What would happen," he asked, "if Will Mersey's dead body, a bullet hole in the back, was found on the floor of the sheriff's office where somebody had thrown it? What if there was a note pinned on the shirt, somethin' that read like this: 'Cattlemen, if you don't want this to happen to you, get out of our way.' What do you reckon would happen?"

"But——"

"Just pretend," Tim insisted. "What would happen?"

"Why, every man in the country, cattleman or not, would be fighting mad," Martha said. "How could they help but be?"

"Mad enough to gang up on Sands?"

"How could they help but be?" Martha repeated, frowning. "But I don't see what you're driving at, Tim."

Tim jerked a thumb over his shoulder, his mouth open to speak, then he said quietly. "This ain't pretty, Martha."

"None of it is. Go on."

"That jasper down the slope there, the gunman. When I first walked up to him I thought it was Will Mersey. His face—well, there's nothin' left of it. But what's left of the rest of him looks like Will Mersey." He paused, watching

Martha. "If he was wearin' Will Mersey's torn clothes I don't reckon anybody would say that it wasn't Will."

Martha did not speak for a moment, only watched him closely. "It's not very pretty, is it? And what would you do with the real Will?"

"I wouldn't. Jeff would. Jeff has got a nice hide-out for me close to the Ox-Bow. It would do just as good for Will Mersey. Don't you see? Will disappears today. Jeff takes him and holds him there at the Ox-Bow. Tonight, this gunman's body is delivered to the sheriff's office. Do you think it would work?"

"You'd only need to keep Will a prisoner long enough to let the ranchers make a martyr out of him. Once they had banded together and struck at Sands, you could let him go, couldn't you?"

"Yes."

Martha sat down across from Tim. There was excitement in her eyes, an excitement that Tim had not seen since that night when he first saw her at the Ox-Bow. It was the excitement of hope.

"It's a risk, Tim," she said quietly.

"Jeff'll take it. I know he will."

"I know so, too."

"But do you think it will work?" Tim insisted.

Martha stood up. "I know it will," she said. "I'm going to saddle up and ride over to the Ox-Bow now. You stay here, Tim. You can't risk being caught now. I'll tell Jeff everything."

"He'll have to toll Will out of town someway, then surprise him and take him."

"He can do it!"

Tim smiled at her excitement. "I reckon you're almost as double-dealin' as I am," he said.

And Martha smiled in return. "If it will save Tornado Basin for us I would stop just short of murder, Tim."

In five minutes Martha rode out of the place and Tim was alone. He set about the unpleasant part of the business now.

Taking an old blanket, he went out to the corral, caught one of the old work horses and was hitching him up to the spring wagon when Curt, Martha's Negro puncher, returned. He was a big fellow, heavily muscled, bowlegged, and the only clue to his age was his gray-shot kinky hair. Ever since Sands had crossed the river Curt had been out riding line for Martha's holdings. It was a form of suicide, Martha had tried to explain to him, for if ever he crossed one of Sands' gunmen in speech or manner he would be shot like a dog. His color was against him to begin with. But the old Negro, who had come into the country with her father, knew his duty and Martha could not dissuade him from it.

A minute's explanation of what Tim was going to do was enough to enlist Curt's help. Together they went down the slope, loaded the body in the wagon, caught up the bay and hid both the horse and the body in the stable. Curt went out again as soon as he had eaten, and Tim was left alone to pass the slowest hours of his life.

Martha had not returned by nightfall, and Tim was beginning to worry. He sat on the doorstep of the darkened house and smoked endless cigarettes. It must have been nine o'clock when he heard the drumming hoofbeats of horses approaching.

It was Martha and Jeff Hardy. Tim lighted the lamp while they unsaddled, and when Martha stepped into the room the dim glow of the lamp was enough to tell Tim that she had met with success. Her face was flushed with color, her eyes snapped with excitement.

When Jeff came in he laid a bundle of clothes on the table and looked long at Tim. "For half the mornin' I was cussin' you so hard I sprained my tongue. Looks like it was a lucky thing you snuck away."

Tim pointed to the clothes and boots, grinning. "Will's?"

"Right," Jeff said. "It was so easy it was almost funny. He told me this mornin' after he'd been to the jail that he figured I'd let you loose. I told him he was welcome to search my place, and he said he aimed to, that he'd be out this afternoon and look for you." He looked over at Martha and grinned down at her, his seamed old face admiring. "When Martha told me about what happened I took your word for it that this dead man would pass for Will. And when Will come we just stuck a gun in his ribs, took his clothes and prodded him up to your hide-out. I've got a couple of the boys guardin' him now."

"How did he take it?"

"Like a cow does dehornin'," Jeff said amiably. "Now, I want a look at your dead deputy out here."

By the light of the lantern Jeff went out with Tim to look at the dead man. He was not a pretty sight, but Jeff looked at him critically and nodded. "I think you got it."

"Then I'll get the clothes."

An hour later the dead gunman, dressed in Will Mersey's artfully torn and soiled clothes, splashed with chicken blood, was lashed to a skittish pack horse. Tim took the lead rope, while Jeff rode alongside. Will Mersey's horse, Jeff informed Tim, had been turned loose, with chicken blood smeared over the saddle and the pastern of his right rear leg. He would drift into town sometime tomorrow.

In the early hours of the morning they rode into Morgan Tanks with the gruesome load. While Jeff kept watch on the deserted street Tim jimmied the lock to the sheriff's office and placed the sprawled figure of the gunman on the floor. The note pinned to his shirt read, "Cattlemen, this is a warning to meddlers!" It was unsigned, but no signature was necessary. Tim left the door open, to be discovered by the earliest riser, and they rode out of town.

"If that don't blow 'em up," Jeff said grimly, "then I hope I die. I hope I don't have to live with a bunch of men who won't fight after that."

7

John Lugan's Fish-hook spread lay south of Jeff Hardy's holdings, but unlike the Ox-Bow, the buildings were not against the foothills. It was watered by the Wagon Tongue, near which the low timber ranch house was located. Its description sounded pleasant enough, when Lugan mentioned it to a stranger, but in reality it was not. For a reason few people understood old man Lugan had shunned the pleasant grove of cottonwoods along the creek, and had built his place against a bare ridge that afforded his stock a shelter of sorts. There were no trees near by, only the low alders along the creek bank, and these had long since been trampled and chewed by the cattle and horses.

When Tip Mahony, Reese Mahony's boy, rode into the place the afternoon of the day Will Mersey's body was found, he saw Lugan getting ready to ride out. Lugan had stopped by the log cookshack to take a package of sandwiches from the cook, and he looked up at Tip's entrance and waved a careless hand. Then he dismounted and waited for Tip, ramming the sandwiches in the pocket of his jeans.

Tip was a wild-eyed young man of twenty whose face could not yet hide his emotions. Before he dismounted from his sorrel, who was breathing as if he had been run hard, he said, "Heard the news, John?"

"If it's about Sands I don't want to," Lugan replied, unsmiling. His heavy face was a little surly, reflecting his distaste for any discussion about sheep.

"Maybe you'll want to hear this," Tip said, irritation crowding into his speech. "It's about Sands, all right."

"Where has he moved now?"

"Plumb into trouble, if you ask me," Tip paused. "Will

Mersey was killed yesterday. They found his body throwed on the floor of the sheriff's office this mornin'. There was a note on it."

"What'd it say?"

" 'Cattlemen, this is a warnin' to meddlers.' "

Lugan looked gravely at the ground. "Well, well," he murmured. "Looks like he means business, don't it?"

"Business!" Tip exploded. "That all you got to say?"

"What do you want me to say?"

"Why, hell, man—that don't leave us no law! It means that damn Sands figures he can walk in here, kill off our law, buy out them rats of nesters and then take over the whole damn Basin!"

"He hasn't done it yet."

"No, by God!" Tip said. "And he won't!" He glared at Lugan with an injured expression. "Hell, man! What they got to do to you to make you fight? You act like I just told you I dropped six bucks at a faro table."

"I don't see much to get proddy about," Lugan replied calmly. "Will Mersey was a fumble-fingered hammerhead that was bound to end up that way. He was a deputy to a nester-sheriff. If they're both out of the way, so much the better."

Tip swallowed hard, as if the words were about to choke him. "Seein' as you feel that way about it, I reckon there's no use of your comin'."

"Where?"

"Over to our place tonight. There's a meetin'. The nesters are comin', too."

"What for?"

"Why, to plan this fight, dammit!" Tip said explosively. "It's root, hog, or die now, Lugan! Hell, what's stoppin' Sands from havin' the whole lot of us beefed? If this county is runnin' under bushwhack law now we might's well plan to fight it, hadn't we?"

"Maybe," Lugan said.

"You comin'?"

"Yeah. I'll stop over. Still, I won't promise to fight the battles of a bunch of nesters."

"Ah-h-h hell!" Tip said in disgust. He wheeled his horse and rode out of the place. Lugan, his face expressionless, mounted and rode toward the mountains. He had to deliver fifty head of beef to Jeff Hardy, in payment for a note, and his men were out rounding up the stuff now.

At the Ox-Bow late that afternoon he found nothing to arouse him. Jeff, as always, was not saying much and that very moderately. Sure, he was going to Mahony's place tonight. Looked like they'd be forced to do something, now that a stranger had figured he could take over a whole county by bushwhack. As to what they'd do about Will's murder, he couldn't tell. Wait and see tonight.

Mahony's place, south of Lugan's, was right in the timber of the foothills. The Mahonys were a large family and had a large house, but its living room scarcely held the men who crowded into it on this night. Not only every single rancher in the Basin was here alongside of the remaining nesters, but a good number of the various crews were here, too. The murder, it was obvious enough, had touched the honor of every cattleman. Martha Kincaid was in one corner and by her stood Tim Enever.

It was the sight of this man that stirred something in Lugan, when he had nodded to those present. He looked at Tim and said, "Decided to show up, now that Mersey's dead?"

"That's about it," Tim agreed. He was smoking, leaning against the wall. His reception here tonight had been mixed. The nesters, through Martha's influence, were convinced that Tim had no share in Borden's murder and that Will Mersey had arrested him to save his face. The big ranchers didn't care anyway, never having believed that Mersey ever did anything right. Today's events, in addition, had put this purely personal fight into the background. It remained for Lugan, however, to drag it up.

"So Mersey's killed the day after you escape jail?" Lugan sneered. "That's considerable coincidence."

Tim, however, was not to be prodded into anger. "I could get redheaded about that, Lugan, if it wasn't so damn easy to prove you're wrong. When I broke jail I came to Miss Kincaid's place in hopes she'd hide me. She did. I haven't been off her place until they brought us news of Mersey's murder."

Lugan looked around at the faces regarding him. "Well?" he challenged.

Jeff Hardy, from his bench by the fireplace, said, "Lugan, I've heard you call Mersey a fool too many times to think you had any respect for his brains. I didn't either." He looked about the room. "Let's get this settled once and for all. This man Enever come here at Borden's request, a complete stranger and a reliable man, as his job shows. Why in tarnation hell would he kill Borden? What possible reason could he have?" He turned to the fireplace and spat accurately into it. "When anybody gives me an answer to that I'm willin' to see this man locked up and stand trial. Until they can we might's well use what help he can give us."

"Which is what?" Lugan said.

"Which is a damn sight more than wearin' out the seat of his pants sittin' around when there's murder been done," Jeff said flatly.

A murmur of assent rose from the men. If they didn't like Tim they at least were willing to tolerate him, which was all he asked. Lugan sat down on a bench near the door and held his Stetson on his lap.

Jeff, as he had always done since any of these men could remember, took over the leadership of the meeting. He cleared his throat and said, "There's just one damn thing this meeting was called for, as I make out. We might as well settle it with no talk." He looked at the nesters and ranchers both. "We got nothin' to fall back on in this county now but our own shootin'. The question is, are we goin' to do it together or singly? And I don't know a better way to put it than this: we're a bunch now, we're together. Whoever wants to back out, let him state his reasons."

"Wait a minute," Lugan said abruptly. "What do you mean, 'we're together'?"

"That was just to start off with," Jeff said calmly. "It's better than startin' off by sayin' we're thirty some men in one room, all with different ideas, ain't it?"

"I'm not together with anyone," Lugan said.

"All right. That makes one of us who ain't goin' to gang up on Sands. Anybody else?" Jeff asked, unperturbed. Shrewdly, he had already assumed that they were joined together to discuss a plan. In one swift move he had caught the tide of their anger at flood and had joined them. "Anybody else want to pull out of our bunch?" he asked.

"I do." This was old Harry Keith, whose place adjoined Mahony to the south. He quarreled with everyone over everything, and long since they had come to accept him as a chronic dissenter. He was a rawboned man, a bachelor, whose disposition had taken on some of the character of his own range, which was dry, rocky and unfavored by nature.

"Yeah, I know you do, Keith," Jeff said dryly. "Ever since I seen you tonight I been tryin' to figure out why you bothered to come. You'd object to Judgment Day, but I'm damned if you'd want to miss the chance to do it in public."

There was general laughter at this. Before Keith could reply, Jeff said, "Well, two out of thirty some ain't so bad." He thereby shut off further dissent, for scarcely a man would have the courage to place himself alongside Keith. Tim, who was a shrewd enough judge of men, smiled faintly at old Jeff's long head. He saw that Jeff had had the patience to wait for the right moment and the ruthlessness to override everyone else when that moment came.

"Well, that ought to stack alongside of Sands' hired gunmen," Jeff observed. "I think he claims about thirty, don't he?"

"He can get more," someone said.

"He'll have to, pretty quick," Jeff observed grimly. That brought another laugh.

"All right, here's the way it shapes up," Jeff said. "Sands has bought out the holdin's of Wiley, Erickson, Worth and McCoy. That gives him a nice stretch along the river, because they all join each other. Since he's movin' north he's bound to move onto Proctor's Circle P range."

"Or Keith's range," Lugan pointed out. "It touches McCoy's."

"Hell with Keith," Jeff said calmly. "He can fight his own battles."

Grimly, Keith nodded and said nothing.

"Then the thing to do is for you nesters to drive your stuff onto Proctor's grass and move over to his place," Jeff said. "Bennett"—he looked at the young, redheaded puncher who was revolving his hat in his hands—"you've got a crew of seven, and your place is close to mine. Send your cook over to Proctor's and throw your boys over to bunk and feed at my place. Mahony, Wallace, Cagle, Rutherford and me will all drive a beef over to Proctor's for butcherin' to feed the lot. Proctor, your men and the nesters and Tim Enever here will patrol your line day and night, in pairs. That's fifteen men you'll have right on the place to meet anything that comes. When anyone sees the first sheep across Proctor's line, call everybody out except one man. Send that man to rouse the rest of us." He looked around. "Anybody got any objection to that?"

"I have," Proctor said. He was a spare little man with a truculent brown face under a pale bald head. "I don't mind puttin' up the nesters at my place, but I'm damned if I'll give 'em grass for their cows."

"Then drive 'em onto my grass," Jeff said quickly. "Anybody got any objections?"

"I got another," Proctor said. "I pay my foreman to work for me, not to lead a fight. Besides that, he don't know how."

"Enever will take over the fightin' end of it," Jeff said.

"That's what he's here for." He looked around the room. "If that's satisfactory I don't see no use in chewin' any more fat."

"I don't see much sense in chewin' this much of it," Lugan said surlily. He picked up his hat, nodded to the group and stepped out.

Jeff laughed. It was all done that simply. Hardly a word had been said about Will Mersey's murder, for old Jeff had been too wise to let that subject come up. If he had let it he knew that immediately sides would have been taken as to Will's actual worth to them, and that would have brought on a wrangling which would have set them against each other and carried over into any following discussion. Now that it was over he let them talk about it, and it was surprising the bitterness these men showed. Many of them had not liked Mersey, had laughed at his blundering ways, his many prejudices. But he had been one of them, a cattleman, and sheepmen did not kill a cattlemen's sheriff—not in this county.

Before the meeting broke up old Jeff came over to Martha. "There's just one thing I didn't say tonight, because it don't concern anybody but you. You're comin' over to the Ox-Bow until all this is finished."

Martha was so delighted with the way the meeting turned out that she agreed. She would move tomorrow.

So Tim Enever found himself the leader of a miscellaneous gang of men who only tolerated each other and were held together by anger. He knew none of them and they did not know him. He had achieved that leadership through shifty politics and because no one else wanted it. Instead of a sheriff and a deputy who placed a loyal band of fighters at his disposal, as had been the prospect when he came to Morgan Tanks, he now had seven paid cowboys and eight halfhearted nesters. He didn't know if they could fight or how, nor if they would take an order or ignore it. He did know that it was a beginning.

8

Proctor's bunkhouse and cookshack were one building, situated a good distance from the high frame house among the live oak trees. At breakfast that morning Tim, who understood that what he would have to fight among these Circle P hands was plain resentment at a stranger's orders, scarcely said a word through breakfast. Afterward, he drifted out to the corral and snaked out his horse, waiting his turn in line.

Joe Manship, the middle-aged foreman, was waiting for him to say something, to assert his authority, but Tim said nothing, waiting.

When he had mounted, ready to ride out, Manship came over to him. "How many of my crew you want this mornin'?" he asked reluctantly.

"None," Tim said.

"I thought you was goin' to patrol the line."

"We are. But I'd like to look at the line first," Tim said.

"Know where it is?"

"I can find it."

Manship turned and called: "Pete." When a young puncher walked over to them Manship ordered him to show Tim the boundary of the Circle P. Manship left then, but not until he studied Tim with a searching expression, as if he were readjusting his judgment. As it happened, Manship had received orders from old man Proctor that the crew was to do nothing but patrol boundary until the nesters had shoved their few head into safe territory and joined them. But Manship, as Tim knew he would, resented having a man over him, even at the old man's orders. It looked, however, as if the stranger was going to mind his own business.

Tim and Pete, Proctor's top hand and a quiet sort of

puncher, rode out southeast, headed for the corner of the
Circle P range. As they passed the first bunch of Circle P
cattle, range beef which were being graded up by registered
stuff, Tim started the talk off on the subject of cows, and
soon Pete was friendly enough.

At the corner marker, a heap of stones close to where
Wagon Tongue Creek swung west again, they turned west.
Now there were sheep in sight occasionally, grazing parallel
with the Circle P line, but a good ways south of it. The
occasional yap of the sheep dogs came to them, and once in
a while a lone rider came into sight and vanished again at
sight of them.

The south boundary was long, and it wasn't till toward
midday that they crossed the road that went past the Circle
P to Morgan Tanks. They were almost out of sight of it,
riding west, when Tim happened to look back and see a
horseman traveling it at a long, mile-eating trot. Tim stood
up in the stirrups and narrowed his eyes. "That's a woman,"
he said to Pete, knowing it was Martha.

"She's in a hurry, too," Pete observed.

"Let's have a look-see." Tim wheeled his sorrel and put
him into a lope, Pete beside him. Presently, when they were
down on the flat, Martha saw them and swerved off the
road.

When she pulled up alongside Tim he said, "Trouble?"

Martha smiled. "Yes—no. Oh, I guess I don't know, Tim.
But Curt saw something this morning that looks funny.
Sands is leaving only a few bands of sheep on this Circle P
south line, and he's moving all the rest across McCoy's
place. He's even bringing more sheep across the river."

"Which corner of McCoy's?"

"Keith's. That's what seems so queer."

Pete drawled, "Almost like he'd been at the meetin' last
night, hunh?" He looked at Tim and Tim nodded slowly.
"Is Curt sure about that, Martha?"

"Positive. They started moving at dawn."

Tim said easily, "Reckon we ought to go over and tell old Keith about it, Pete?"

"Won't do no harm."

They talked a little longer and then Martha left. She was headed for the Ox-Bow, and Curt was following with her few belongings, after he had driven the cattle off.

After she had gone Pete lifted his hat and scratched a mop of black hair. "Movin' in on Keith. He ain't doin' that by accident; somebody told him about Keith." He looked sharply at Tim. "Some of them nesters might not be so willin' to fight as they are to make money," he said quietly.

"Give 'em a chance," Tim said. "We don't know yet."

They wasted no time, going back the way they had come and on through Keith's range. He was to the east of Proctor's Circle P, between it and the mountains, and the land was slowly tilting to a bench as they progressed. It was drier country here, and more rock, intersected by shallow canyons. It was the least choice range of the whole Tornado Basin, Pete said, since all the creeks missed it, and Keith had to depend entirely on scattered water holes.

The house itself on the floor of a wide canyon was backed by a bare butte of the timberless foothills, and was built of stone. Sagging pole corrals flanked a barn built of slab lumber off to the south, and the place looked hot and treeless, bare as it was of grass or any green growth. The afternoon shadow of the butte was crawling toward it, promising coolness.

They sloped down off the bench and took the short road to the house. Old man Keith had seen them coming, and he stood in the doorway of his place, a carbine leaning against the jamb.

"Howdy, Keith," Pete greeted him.

"If you're after help from me you won't get it," Keith said ungraciously.

Pete grinned and looked at Tim. "Ain't he a pleasant cuss?" he remarked. "I got a notion to ride off and let him find out for himself."

"Find out what?" Keith asked.

"Don't you keep an eye on them sheep?" Peter asked.

"No. There's only me here and I'm kept busy without sashayin' around watching Sands."

"Well, from now on you can watch Sands without any sashayin'," Pete said bluntly. "His sheep are on your land."

Keith looked at him suspiciously. "Who said so?"

Pete kept his temper and replied that Martha Kincaid's Curt had seen them. Keith replied he didn't believe a damn nigger. From there the argument waxed warm. Pete, who had the wisdom not to be angry, now started to string old man Keith along, contradicting everything he said and prodding him into real anger. Tim had long since lost interest, and he looked around the place and down the valley. Suddenly, his glance settled on four black pinpoints down on the canyon floor. They were riders, he made out.

He interrupted Pete. "Those your men comin', Keith?"

"I told you I didn't have any crew," Keith said shortly. He looked down the valley.

"That's Sands, comin' to pay a call on you," Pete taunted. "We'll stick around and help you out, old man."

"I don't need any help," Keith said stubbornly. "Get the hell away from me and let me be."

"I'd like to hear what they say, if it's Sands' men." Pete insisted.

"I'll talk to 'em alone. I'll not have 'em thinkin' I'm callin' on anybody for help."

"All right. We'll pull our horses in behind the house and come inside and listen," Pete offered.

"Suits me. Only don't show yourself. This is my business." The old man spat stubbornly.

Tim and Pete led their horses behind the house and tied them. Then they went inside. The room they entered was dirt floored with only the crudest of furniture. It fitted in with the hard-bitten cantankerous ways of the old man.

Keith stood in the doorway and waited, while Tim and Pete, behind burlap curtains, watched the four men ride into the yard. They were Sands' riders, all right, rough and un-shaven men who looked at the place with sneering contempt.

Their leader was a long-faced clean-shaven man in a checked cotton shirt. He pulled up his horse in front of Keith and crossed his arms on the saddle horn, looking around the place with deliberate insolence and finally bringing his gaze to bear on the old man.

"It ain't much," he drawled, "but I reckon it'll do us."

"Do you for what?" Keith asked bluntly.

"For headquarters," the man said. "You better start movin' out, old man."

The insolence of the man almost took Keith's breath away. With an effort he controlled himself. "I didn't know I'd sold the place."

"You ain't," the man replied. "You just lost it. We're takin' over."

"You Sands' men?"

"That's right. Now you go get what you want to take along, then saddle up your pony and drift, mister."

"No damn saddle bum is going to move me off this place!" Keith said. "Now get the hell out of here while you can still ride, all of you!"

The man was sideways to him, his right hand hidden. Keith was holding the carbine across his chest, so that he could easily bring it to bear on the four of them.

The speaker turned to his mates and said, "Hear that?" And then, without waiting for an answer, without straightening up from his leaning position, suddenly he brought his gun into sight across the saddle horn.

Keith understood the move too late. He had been watching the man's head, not his hand. He yanked his carbine up shoulder high, just as the rider's six gun exploded three times in rapid succession. Old Keith shot once at the sky, and made a wild grab for the doorjamb and missed. He sprawled on his back on the dirt floor.

Tim whipped up his six gun, crashed the glass of the

window with it, and before the glass touched the ground he had shot. The rider gave a savage yank at his reins, rearing his horse, and then he sloped out of the saddle into the dirt.

Pete knelt in the doorway, both guns blazing. The attack had caught the others unawares. One of them folded up over his saddle horn before he could draw his gun.

The second swung down behind his pony's neck, Indian-fashion, and rammed his spurs into his horse. Tim shot the horse before he could move and the rider leaped clear. The third man was pulling his horse away, gouging his flanks and shooting wildly at the house. Tim ran out into the open now, both guns silent, and made a dive for the downed horse. From there he took careful aim at the second man and shot once. On the heel of his shot, Pete opened up on him too, and the man's body jerked as if he were being poked by some invisible stick.

The third man had fled now; he thundered out of the yard, crouched over the back of his horse. Both Tim and Pete took long shots at him, but for several long seconds it seemed as if they had missed. Then the man began to sag sideways, and before his horse had taken a dozen more steps he had slid out of the saddle and rolled over and over on the ground, coming to a stop against the watering trough by the corral.

The acrid smell of powder smoke filled the air. Tim stepped in the doorway just as Pete was rising. Through the lazy drift of smoke, they could make out a half-dozen riders pounding up the valley toward them.

"We better drift," Pete said laconically.

Tim knelt by Keith, feeling for his heartbeat, but the stubborn old man had been dead before he hit the ground. Tim stepped over him and out the door. Pete had suddenly sat down, and on his jean leg was a long smear of blood.

"Shuck out of here while you can," Pete said quietly. "I can't move. Just leave me your gun."

For answer, Tim went behind the house and came back with both horses. "Where you hit?"

"The leg."

"Grit your teeth, boy, because you go," Tim murmured. He reached down and lifted Pete's slight body; then, as if it were a sack of oats, he hoisted it into the saddle. Pete gave a low groan and clutched wildly at the saddle horn, then steadied himself.

"Come along," Tim said. "Can you hang on?"

"Yeah. Go on up the canyon," Pete said, between gritted teeth.

Tim brought his reins down over the rump of Pete's horse. Lurching in the saddle, doing the best he could to hang on, and too sick to care much, Pete stuck to the saddle like a burr. Tim did his profane best to stampede Pete's horse, shooting twice at his heels in the effort.

Finally, in pure panic, Pete's horse stretched out. Just as they rounded the lip of the butte, the first shot from the pursuers kicked up a geyser of sand beside Tim.

Once in the upper canyon, they were safe, but Tim did not know how long they would be. The walls were narrowing, crowding in on them, and they were impossibly steep. If it was a box canyon they would have to make a stand and fight.

But Pete's horse, like a frightened rabbit, was keeping well ahead of Tim's. At last, when the walls got so narrow that Tim gave up hope of a way out, he put the spurs to his horse and pulled alongside Pete's roan. He caught the roan's bridle and pulled him to a halt. Pete was slumped down over the horn, holding onto it till his hands were white.

Roughly, Tim yanked his head up and slapped his face. "Pete! Pete!" he said savagely.

Pete opened eyes sick with pain.

"There a way out of this canyon?"

"Go on," Pete mumbled. "There's a turnoff almost at the end."

Taking the reins of Pete's horse, Tim went ahead. The canyon was crowding in on them, until there was scarcely room for a wagon. And the steep end of the canyon came into sight and Tim's heart sank. Evidently Pete hadn't had any idea where he was.

But on closer inspection, there was a knifelike slit on the left wall. It was just big enough to allow for a horse. Already now the shouts of Sands' riders were echoing in the bottleneck. Tim led Pete's horse to the mouth of the slit and slashed him savagely across the rump. The horse, terrified, plunged into the slit, and Tim followed. Twice it looked as if they were crowded into a wedge which would trap them, and twice Pete's horse, harried by Tim's rope end, rammed through, scraping Pete's leg on the wall. In another forty yards the walls started to fall away.

As they came out of the slit, a startled cow shied away from them, heading up the canyon. At once, Tim abandoned Pete and lifted his pony into a gallop. He raced past the cow, circled and came back at her.

Pete's tired horse was stopped now, standing by the side of the canyon. He did not so much as move as Tim hazed the cow past him and back into the wedge. Again Tim entered that narrow file, the cow plunging ahead of him. And again he could hear the shouts of Sands' riders as they worked toward him through the slit. When they came to the place where Pete's horse had balked at the narrowness, the cow stopped.

Tim drew his gun and, holding it on one hand, he snapped his rope end at the cow with the other. The cow made a lunge to get through the crack, and then Tim shot. He emptied his gun at her, and she sagged down into the wedge, its narrow walls almost supporting her erect. It was a plug, anyway, and it would serve to stop pursuit.

Tim backed his pony out, taking a long time in the process. But he was rewarded by the angry shouts of Sands' men as they came upon the dead cow blocking their path.

Once in the wide canyon, Tim saw that Pete had fallen off his pony. He lay face down in the sand, and his horse stood by him, head down.

Examination showed that he was still alive. Two wicked

wounds in his thigh, one above the other, were already caked with blood, and the flow of it was stopped.

Tim hoisted the unconscious figure into the saddle in front of him. The pain of it roused Pete, and he raised his head, finally focusing his eyes on Tim who was on the ground, holding him.

Pete smiled faintly. "All right, partner?"

"All right," Tim grinned. "We're headin' home."

Pete murmured, "Tim, you'll do to ride the river with," and then his head slumped on his chest.

Riding double, they pulled into the Circle P at midnight. Old Proctor and Manship and a half dozen nesters besides the crew were there when Pete was lifted off Tim's horse and taken into the main house.

Later, when Tim had washed up and was sitting before his meal in the bunkhouse Proctor came back and demanded the full story. Briefly, Tim told him, omitting any mention of his saving Pete.

"That all?" Proctor asked harshly when he was finished. Tim nodded.

"It is not," Proctor said gently. "Pete come to when we washed his leg. He told me how you wouldn't leave him in that jam there at Keith's. He don't know yet how you pulled him out of it."

Color crept into Tim's face as Proctor told the assembled men what Pete had told him. Nobody said anything, but Tim knew that from now on he was one of them.

It wasn't until later that Proctor took him off into the night on pretext of looking at Pete's horse.

"I just wanted to know somethin'," Proctor said, looking up at Tim in the uncertain moonlight. "Don't it strike you that Sands' move today was timed pretty good—almost like he knew that we wouldn't be there to help old Keith make his fight?"

"It looks mighty like it," Tim agreed.

"In other words, somebody there at Mahony's last night told Sands what passed there."

Again Tim agreed.

"You wouldn't be making any guesses, would you?" Proctor asked slowly.

"No. Only one thing I'm damn sure of," Tim said quietly. "Neither you nor your men like these nesters. You're only toleratin' 'em now. If there's any blame due you'll put it on them, won't you?"

"I'd plumb admire to," Proctor agreed frankly.

"Don't," Tim said briefly. "One wrong word now and you're likely to swing 'em all over to Sands. If they think we don't trust 'em, they're gone. And whoever is sellin' out to Sands is bound to be trapped sooner or later. Let it ride and keep your eyes open."

"Maybe you're right," Proctor said reluctantly. "I reckon you've earned the right to run this your way."

Tim breathed an inaudible sigh of relief and remarked that he was tired, bringing the conversation to an end—and safely.

9

The yard of Keith's place was spotted with piles of tarp-covered goods, the food and ammunition and stores of Warner Sands' small army. The stove had been moved out into the yard, and a tarp stretched over two long deal tables to serve as the cookshack. Ponies were always clustered around the watering trough out by the corral, and men came and went at all hours of the day and night. They had been here three days now, and under the closest sort of guard fifteen thousand sheep had crossed the Tornado bridge, cut across Wiley's and McCoy's old places and had moved in on the poor and almost waterless range of Keith's.

Julie Sands, riding a little ahead of the same still-faced, alert-looking puncher who had fallen in with her as she came out of the sheriff's office, looked at it with obvious distaste. It was familiar in a way; only the setting and the faces were different. It was just another one of those temporary camps to be deserted tomorrow for the new place that her father would take over.

The puncher pulled up beside her and said, "I'll see if he's busy, Miss Julie."

"Do," Julie said wearily. That morning at her hotel she had been roused at sunup and summoned by this same puncher to visit her father.

At her entrance to the shack, two men took off their hats, glanced at Sands and got his nod of dismissal, then left. The smell in here was as rank as a goat sty, Julie thought, as her nose wrinkled in distaste. Save for a table, two chairs and a lamp, the room was bare, with its single window showing broken panes.

Warner Sands stood up at her entrance and smiled faintly, indicating a chair.

"You're sure I won't get mange if I sit down in it?" Julie asked coldly. Suddenly she burst out. "Dad, why do you have to do this? You aren't living with these men, are you?"

"Hardly."

"How do you come to be here in this—this pigsty?"

"My men took it over," Sands said cryptically. "Sit down, Julie."

Julie did. She was wearing a brown riding habit with divided skirt, and she crossed her legs and put her hat on her knee.

"I'm afraid you're going to have to leave Morgan Tanks," Sands began. A worried frown creased his brow. He toyed with his knife and used those swift irritable motions that told Julie he was keyed up with some excitement.

"That's fine. Do you expect me to complain?"

"No. Only events make it necessary. The ranchers think I murdered their deputy."

"I don't want to hear it," Julie replied swiftly. "Where are you sending me now?"

Sands tapped the table with the knife. "That's it. I hate to tell you."

"Then it's not St. Louis?"

"Definitely not!" Sands said sharply. "I thought we had that all settled long since."

"You have," Julie replied. "I haven't. I can always keep trying."

Sands made an impatient gesture. "No. This town is up in the Tornadoes. It's not a town, really, but an old logging camp. There's a hotel there and several houses, I think. It'll be pretty rough."

"That's what you want, isn't it?"

Sands smiled patiently. "Honey, don't ride me so much. When I get this job done we'll be settled for good. I have our house picked out for us already—the Ox-Bow. Do you think you'll like this valley?"

"I'll love it," Julie said bitterly. "With your gunmen filling the town, ready to shoot the first man who doesn't tip his hat to me, why shouldn't I?"

Sands drew a deep breath, his signal that he was through arguing. "St. Cloud," he said firmly, "will take you up there today. Peavey isn't much of a town, but it'll have to do."

"St. Cloud?" Julie said, her dark eyes flashing. "Does he have to take me?"

"Don't you like him?"

"Like him? I loathe him! I'm afraid he'll shoot me every time I turn my back!"

Again Sands drew a deep breath in an effort to control his temper. "I've had St. Cloud take care of you because he's a little different stripe than the rest of these men. He's loyal, he's clean and he's a good man. If you prefer anyone else, say so."

"They are all alike," Julie said indifferently. "Only some day I hope to talk with a man who doesn't jump at his own shadow, who isn't afraid to go in a dark room, and who doesn't have to have his back to a wall and his face to a door every time he sits down."

"I'm running sheep," Sands pointed out dryly. "If I have to employ that stripe of man it's through no choice of my own."

Julie ignored this because she had heard it offered as his apology for everything—the way they lived, the people they knew, the friendliness they couldn't buy and for the animosity they stirred up. Sands' hide was thick, impervious; but she was young and wanted friendship—or at least she had, until she saw it was useless.

"When do I start?"

"Now. Today. There's going to be trouble in this valley and I don't want you mixed in it."

"I thought these ranchers wouldn't fight."

"My information is that they intend to," Sands said grimly. "I'm paying well for that information. It had better be correct." He thought he would not mention the fact that he had already lost four men in a fight.

"Is it Tim Enever?" Julie asked.

Sands was surprised at that name on her lips. It was almost as if she had read his mind. "Yes, he's leading it. Who told you?"

"He did."

"When?"

"I visited him when he was in jail. I explained to him how you were not to blame for his being arrested, that you couldn't possibly be."

"That was kind of you," Sands said gently, almost ironically, "but hardly necessary. I'd prefer you didn't see him again."

"Unless he comes, to—what is it, Peavey?—I'll hardly have the chance," Julie replied indifferently.

Sands rose. "Well, you might as well be off. I've got a man up there and I've made careful inquiries about everything. You'll be safe enough, and comfortable, I think. There's a half-breed Ute woman there, the wife of the hotel keeper, so you'll have somebody to do your clothes and such."

A man stepped through the door, saw Julie and then caught the irritation in Sands' face and stepped out again. Julie rose and kissed her father perfunctorily. Suddenly, facing him, she leaned against him and gathered the lapels of his coat in her hands and said passionately, "I don't wish you any bad luck, Dad, but I hope they beat you! I hope they drive you back over the mountains and kill every sheep you have! I hope they take every dollar you have to your name!"

Sands said quietly, a little sternly, "That's a strange wish for a man's daughter to make."

"But I do!" Julie insisted. "I think when that's done you'll come to your senses and forget this mania." She paused, watching her father's face. "Dad, aren't you content with what we've got now? You're a rich man, you know."

"Run along," Sands said briefly. "If you need anything, ask for it."

Julie turned, resignation in her face, and went outside. St. Cloud was holding a horse for her, a fresh one, one of the many that were absolutely gentled for her at Sands' orders.

Sands watched her ride off, and then turned his attention to the man waiting for him. "What is it, Muller?" It was his sheep foreman, a man a few years his junior, with the round close-cropped head of a German storekeeper. He wore a black suit and townsmen's scuffed shoes. But more than anything else setting him apart from the others was the derby hat he wore on the back of his head. Rain and sun had faded it to a green color, just as they had faded his eyes to a watery, bleached blue. He knew more about sheep than any man alive, Sands believed, and he lived for them. A peaceable man, he did not concern himself with Sands' quarrels; he watched the sheep, their condition, their lambing, their grass and their water. He wore a gun in a shoulder holster. Nobody had ever seen him use it except to threaten a careless herder.

"Same thing in the north," Muller said, his speech slow. "Face the facts, chief. You haven't got half enough water, not a fourth enough, not an eighth enough."

"Can't those springs be dug out and freshened?"

"No. There's just not enough water. By tonight you'll have close to twenty thousand head on this piece."

"I don't give a damn about their condition," Sands said impatiently. "All I want is for them to have an appetite."

"You don't understand. They'll die here in a week."

"Why? Can't you take turn about watering them?"

Muller was patient. "The way it stands now, you can water a bare fifth of them once a day. A drink every five days is not enough, Sands."

"Meaning I've got to move?"

"Yes. Only get out of here while your sheep will still drive."

Sands' eyes narrowed a little. "I'm not going back a foot, I tell you. That river doesn't exist as far as we're concerned."

"Then go somewhere else."

"Have you seen that crowd on Proctor's line?" Sands asked dryly.

Muller shrugged. "That's not my business. But if you don't get these sheep off here within three days you never will move them."

Sands stared down the canyon, his face thoughtful. "You say those springs can't be cleaned out? Have you tried?"

"Yes."

"Then try again. I'll get a couple of men and go out with you tonight. Tomorrow we'll have a try at it."

He called out to a puncher at the corrals and told him to saddle a horse. To three other riders waiting for him Sands gave instructions to get tools and join him, and then he mounted and rode out of the place with Muller. The three men, spades and picks on a pack horse, followed behind them.

The water hole Muller chose for his demonstration was

not far from Proctor's line. It was little more than a ground seep at the base of a limestone outcrop occurring at the foot of a steep ridge. A tank had been dug long since by Keith, but its sides had been tramped down by the constant milling of the sheep. Small bands of them were being cut out from the main herds to be brought to this water, which was little more than a thin soup of mud.

Sands regarded it from the top of the ridge and then gave orders to keep the sheep away. He went down to look at the spring.

"You say you've dug this out?" he asked Muller.

"The sheep have tramped it in again."

Sands turned to his crew. "All right, get to work. Clean it out at the base of that rock." He stood there watching, smoking impatiently, giving orders, until the sun went down and it was too dark to work.

"Where's the nearest camp?" he asked Muller.

Muller told him it was less than a half mile south, and Sands announced that they'd put up there for the night and get to work early in the morning. He looked preoccupied as he rode into the camp and accepted the supper of mutton, coffee and pan bread offered him. A herder and three riders made up this camp. Sands ignored them, and took his food a little ways away from the fire. The work this afternoon had been disappointing, and it looked as if Muller was right. They'd have to move off this range. But where? The thought of going back to the river and giving up what he had already won was distasteful to him. It was more than that; it was impossible. He saw his mistake now. It was in moving so many sheep onto Keith's poor range.

Still, he reflected, this was part of the technique of taking over a range. Move your men onto a place, then bring your sheep in immediately. By the time the other side was ready for action the obstacles looked insurmountable to them. The average cowman had no idea of how to move sheep off a range. He could only try to destroy them—and that was harder than it looked, especially when he had to drive off a crew of fighting men before he could get to the sheep.

But nevertheless he had made a mistake here, Sands reflected. If, by tomorrow noon, they weren't able to produce a good flow of water from these springs they would have to move. He took his plate back to the fire and lighted his pipe, scowling into the flames. He was thinking of those men riding Proctor's line. Everywhere you looked on the Circle P boundary there was a pair of riders watching you.

Sands turned in, feeling low in spirit. A daring move was necessary, but just what that move would be he was not yet sure. The crew turned in, too, leaving one guard and the sheepherder awake.

Silence fell over the camp. The sheep, down in the hollow of the small valley where they were bedded, finally forgot their thirst and settled down for the night. Only an occasional complaint from the lambs disturbed the night silence. The sheep dog, his day's work over, listened attentively for any disturbing sounds, then moved in close to the fire and curled up in its circle of dying warmth. The day was over.

The herder, a Mexican, presently wrapped himself in his blankets. Only the guard, a pale-faced puncher in middle years, stayed awake, and he picked up a stick and began to whittle idly. He never knew how much time had passed before the dog raised his head, looked across the fire, and began to growl.

"Quit it!" the puncher said sharply.

The dog ignored him. He came to his feet, his hackles rising, and growled savagely. The guard struck at him with a stick, and the dog dodged. Idly, then, the guard turned to see what had disturbed the dog.

Tim Enever was standing just inside the circle of firelight, his two guns trained on the guard.

They looked at each other for a long moment, and then Tim drawled softly, "Better shut that dog up. Stand up, you."

The guard came to his feet, his hands over his head. He

aimed a kick at the dog, who immediately began to bark. The herder wakened, saw the guard, and his gaze traveled to Tim. He, too, came to his feet, his hands in the air. This was the way the camp wakened, and Sands was the last to arouse.

He sat up in his blankets, looking irritable and only half awake. And then he, too, saw the three guards, the three punchers, the herder and Muller, all standing facing Tim, their hands raised.

Tim was looking at him when he turned his head. Sands made a movement to get up and Tim said, "Sit still, Sands. I don't aim to take long."

Deliberately, he squatted on his heels, his back against a tree, his guns resting on his knees, and waited for someone to speak.

"Did you want to talk to me?" Sands asked irritably.

"Not especially," Tim replied cheerfully. The good nature in his voice was belied by his eyes. They were sultry, and little dancing lights which might have been the reflection of the fire played in them.

"Then what do you want here?" Sands asked sharply. "If you're going to shoot anyone, then get it over with. If you aren't, what do you want?"

"Ever hear dynamite, Sands?" Tim drawled.

"Of course. Why?"

"Then listen to some more," Tim went on. "In a few minutes your spring will be buried under fifty ton of rock."

Sands turned a little pale at this news, but his face did not betray him. "Blowing it up, eh?"

"All of 'em," Tim said briefly. "No more water, Sands."

A rumbling explosion from over the ridge came to them; it was followed by a shaking of the earth, as if rock or dirt had started a long slide. Tim grinned at the noise; Sands' face did not change a particle.

He said to Tim, "Maybe you won't have such an easy time with the other springs."

"Maybe," Tim conceded. "If we got only three or four of them it'll be enough, won't it?"

Suddenly, Sands smiled. "More than enough, I should say. But if you'd talked to me first I could have saved you the trouble of doing it."

Tim looked interested. "How's that?"

"There's not enough water here at best, not even with all the springs."

"So you'd have had to move anyway?"

"That's it," Sands said. He and Tim regarded each other levelly and for a long moment, each trying to guess what the other was thinking.

"Where to?" Tim said at last.

"I think," Sands said slowly, "I'll move over onto Proctor's. I like the idea of that creek."

"You can always try," Tim murmured. "Of course, we may argue a little with you."

Sands nodded absently. "I like the idea of that creek," he repeated thoughtfully. "Down at the southeast corner of the Circle P it makes a bend toward this range. I think that's where I'll come over."

The audacity of the man confounded and angered Tim. He wondered if he was serious. He had known men whose arrogance goaded them into forewarning an enemy of their next move, then going ahead with it. There was a certain Bill Bonney, down South in Lincoln County, New Mexico, who was fond of that trick. Moreover, he made it work. Tim laughed softly, unpleasantly.

"You know, Sands, I'm glad I met you," he drawled.

Sands smiled meagerly. "Don't let your anger prod you into saying something you'll regret."

"I don't reckon I'll regret sayin' this," Tim said quietly. "I said I'm glad you and me are locking horns. You see, you ain't ever been licked the way I lick a man. And I ain't ever licked a man with as big a head as you wear. I'm goin' to do an extra-big job of whippin' you, I think. I just don't like the way you curl your tail."

"I've heard that brag before," Sands said quietly. "I'll show you where you're mistaken. In the first place, you love to talk. Any man that talks instead of acts isn't a born fighter. Now you take me. Do you know what I'd do if I were in your place right now and you were in mine?"

"You'd probably shoot me."

"Exactly," Sands murmured. "I would have already discovered that you are the leader of the men opposing me. If I had a chance like yours I'd pull the trigger and remove my trouble. But you won't, will you?"

Tim stood up, barely able to control himself. "I might, if I don't clear out of here pretty quick," he said thickly.

Sands laughed noiselessly. "I can give you a piece of advice, Enever, that you won't take. It's the best advice anybody ever gave a man."

"Go ahead."

"Have the courage of your ambition. That's all you need."

Tim said quietly, "I don't know which smells worse, Sands, you or your sheep. I think you do."

He stepped backwards out of the circle of firelight and disappeared into the night. One of the gunmen whipped out his gun and leaped over the fire in pursuit. Sands said sharply, "Come back here, Abe!"

The man checked himself, and turned to his boss. They were all looking at him, waiting for orders. Sands pulled on his boots and stood up, facing Muller. "How far can these sheep be driven?"

"One day hard," Muller said. "Maybe into the night for six hours with this moon."

Sands wheeled to the others. "Abe, I want you to ride over to the cabin and pick up Dillman, Sholes, Parkhurst and Minor. They're to ride north into those badlands that separate this range from Mahony's. I want them to find at least four trails through those badlands that lead to Roan Creek on Mahony's land. I want them to report to me at that north water hole by four this afternoon."

"But Sands!" Muller said swiftly. "There's not a drop of water in those badlands!"

"Don't I know it?" Sands said irritably. "I'm not stopping there. I'm driving through them. If these sheep can travel for eighteen hours that's time enough!" He glared at Muller. "Isn't it?"

Muller nodded slowly. "Yes—if there's water at the end of it."

"There will be!" Sands said grimly. "That fool of an Enever will go back to the Circle P, and by mid-day tomorrow he'll have every able-bodied man outside of Morgan Tanks strung along the Wagon Tongue waiting for our rush to water. I'll send ten men down there to throw lead at them and hold them there. Meanwhile, I'll have moved these sheep north clean off this damn barren range onto a new one. And once we're on Mahony's grass we're there to stay!"

Without waiting for Muller's shrug he turned to another rider. "Mort, you'll do some tall riding tonight. I want you to rouse every camp and have their herds moving by daylight toward the badlands. Take the south herds first." To the last guard he said, "I want the guard on the Circle P line doubled. I don't want any strange riders snooping on this range today. Shoot any stranger. Now be off, all of you!"

He turned to the Mexican. "Juan, start this herd moving two hours before dawn." And to Muller, he said more gently, almost musingly, "Cheer up, Gus. I've pulled you through worse ones than this."

"But every mile you put between my sheep and that river hurts," Muller said doubtfully. "You know there's water back there. What about ahead?"

"I know there's water there!" Sands flared.

"But can we get to it?"

"We've got to! Hear, man? We've got to!" More quietly he added, "Yes, we can."

10

When Tim faded back into the night, leaving Sands' camp, he was laughing quietly. He was still laughing when he mounted his horse and listened for any sign of pursuit.

That was once Warner Sands had overplayed his hand. He was going to make a try for water at the Wagon Tongue, was he? He was not. He was going to make a try for Mahony's water through the badlands, and that lie about the thrust at the creek was born of desperation. That desperation had been manufactured by Tim and the ranchers through the blowing up of these water holes. And that move had been dictated by Tim's iron belief that Sands would not go back when he could go ahead. Tim had talked these ranchers into staking their all on his hunch that Sands would move through the badlands. Tonight's talk with Sands had convinced him that his hunch was right.

Joe Manship and John Lugan were waiting for him beyond the water hole. Lugan's presence here tonight was the result of a simple plan adopted by the ranchers. From now on they were to work in threes and travel in threes. In this way they acted as a check on each other. No man, whoever he was, could get to Sands with information if he was watched by two others. Lugan, who was informed that he would be told nothing unless he submitted to this plan, had reluctantly agreed and thrown in his lot with the other ranchers. His presence here tonight was under protest; he had sneered at Tim's plan.

"Any trouble?" Manship asked, as Tim joined them and they started off west.

Tim told them of his meeting with Sands and what Sands had threatened.

"He'll do it, too," Lugan said, when Tim was finished.

Manship said, "How you figure that, John?"

Lugan laughed shortly. "By common sense—something there's damn little of around here."

Tim, however, did not rise to the bait. He let Manship take the burden of the conversation, contenting himself with listening. Presently Manship said, "You think he'll strike at the creek, like he said?"

"He's always done what he said he would, hasn't he?" Lugan countered surlily. "He said he'd bring sheep in here. He has. He said he'd cross the river. He did. He told Keith, in Enever's hearing, that he was going to move in on Keith's range. He did." He looked over at Tim. "To my way of thinkin', Sands isn't smart. He's just tough—and plain as water."

"Your opinion don't matter a damn, Lugan," Tim said quietly. "It's already settled what we'll do."

"Sure. All you got to do is wait and see if I'm right."

In another hour they came to the Circle P boundary and immediately picked up two riders. Tim related what had passed that night, told them to take the news back to the men waiting at the Circle P and to start hunting their positions in the badlands under cover of darkness. The riders who had gone onto Keith's range to blow in the water holes would all be returned by daylight. They were to fort up at the bend of Wagon Tongue Creek, just in case Sands really meant what he said.

When Tim was through giving instructions Lugan said, "Why are you tellin' them? I thought we were ridin' back to the Circle P."

"No," Tim said. "We're headin' for the Ox-Bow."

"What's over there?"

"You'll have to wait and see," Tim said.

Lugan, however, was stubborn. "This travelin' in threes is all right," he said sourly, "when you're all goin' the same place. But I don't happen to want to go to the Ox-Bow. So good night, gents."

"Wait a minute," Tim said softly. "Where you goin'?"

"Back to the Circle P and sleep."

"I don't think you are," Tim said mildly. "I'll admit you could ride back to the Circle P with those boys. But in a couple of hours they'll all scatter to their positions there in the badlands. Since you're supposed to fort up with us two that means that you'll have to hunt us alone. And no man is allowed to ride this range alone, from now on."

Lugan said nothing for a moment. Then he pulled his horse over to a place beside Tim's.

"I got a notion you think maybe I'm the man that sold out to Sands," he said thickly.

"I didn't say so, did I?"

"It's plain enough without."

"You're gettin' the same treatment all of us are."

"That's where you're wrong," Lugan said grimly. "Maybe those others are suckers enough to let you bluff 'em. But you don't run any sandys on me, Enever. I'm leavin'."

There was a soft whisper of metal on leather, and Tim's gun glinted dully in the moonlight. "Lugan," he said gently, "I've never liked you. I don't like your damn cross-grained ways. If you move another ten feet in that direction I'll fix you up so you can't ride."

Lugan sat there facing him for a full ten seconds, trying to gauge the tone of his voice. There must have been a warning in it, for he made no attempt to move. "Put it at the end of a gun and it don't leave me much choice," he said finally.

"Put it at the end of two guns," Joe Manship said quietly, firmly. "You come in with us on that agreement, Lugan. It's too late to back out now."

Lugan only shrugged. Tim touched his horse and they headed north for the three hours' ride to the Ox-Bow, and not once during that ride did Lugan comment.

There were lights burning at the Ox-Bow when they arrived, for the crew had only just left for the badlands, after a quick breakfast. Jeff and Martha greeted them, and there was anxiety in Martha's face.

While Charlie rustled up breakfast for them Tim told of his conversation with Sands that night. Lugan sat in surly silence, waiting for his breakfast. Tim took one cup of coffee, then rose and went out. Jeff, at a sign from him, followed.

There seemed to be an agreement between them which did not need speech. Jeff got his lantern and they went up the ridge to the foundation of the old house. Two men with rifles came out to meet them; they were the guards which had been with Mersey night and day since his capture.

Jeff spoke to them and then went down into the cellar, Tim following. At their entrance, Will Mersey, on a cot near the side wall, roused sleepily.

Jeff set the lantern on the floor. "I've come to give you your last chance, Will," he said. "Wake up and listen."

"I'm awake," Will growled.

"The water holes are blowed up and the men are on their way to the badlands now," Jeff said. "Either it'll work or it won't. You want to help us, instead of sittin' here sulkin'?"

Will scratched his piebald hair and grunted. "Hell, yes, I want to help you."

"All you got to do to get out of here is give your word you'll let Tim alone and not try and arrest him," Jeff said implacably. He stared down at Will. He was so tall that he was almost half bent to miss the ceiling, and it gave him a threatening look, almost as if he were going to pounce on the deputy.

Will looked from Jeff to Tim and back to Jeff again. "If I don't, how long you goin' to keep me here, Jeff?"

"Till this thing is settled and Tim is out of the country," Jeff said grimly. "Take your choice, Will. You was kidnapped and that gunman put in your office because we reckoned it was the last chance to get us all workin' together. It worked, all right. Tonight we got every cattleman in the county ready to fight. All that's keepin' you here is your damn stubbornness."

Will scrubbed his face with the flat of his hand, his brow wrinkled. Suddenly he looked up at Jeff. "You got my word, Jeff. But the only reason I'm doin' it is because I want a chance at Sands."

"Git dressed then," Jeff said. "The boys have already started."

Later, at the house, Will's reception by Manship and Lugan was strange to behold. At Will's entrance, Manship rose out his chair as if he'd seen a ghost. Lugan took it more calmly, looking from Tim to Jeff for an explanation. When it was forthcoming, Manship agreed that it had been wise. Lugan only looked at Tim and said, "I've heard of men bein' so sharp they cut their own throat."

Five minutes later, when Will had gulped a cup of coffee, they left the Ox-Bow for the badlands. At bare dawn they forded Roan Creek, the southern boundary of Mahony's range, and entered the broken country.

These badlands were an upended tangle of deep canyons, climbing into the foothills on the east and deep into Proctor's range on their western edge. They were seven miles wide as the crow flies, but once in the labyrinthine canyons, the distance through was almost tripled. There were three trails through it, easily distinguishable by the tracks of cattle who moved from water on the one side to the grass on the other. Of the three, Tim and his crew had drawn the east wall of the middle trail. Another quartet of ranchers was now approaching the west wall by a different route, so as to minimize the likelihood of discovery.

Jeff, who knew these badlands before any other white man had seen them, led off, avoiding the main trail and taking to the side canyons. They gradually worked their way deep into the maze of twisting tortuous canyons, climbing walls, sliding down steep slopes, picking their way over ground so rough their horses almost balked.

Hour after hour Jeff led the way deeper and higher into

that upended tangle. At last, toward mid-day, he drew up in a small rincon and pointed to a low flat-topped butte to the south. "That's our place. From here on we walk."

It took them another hour to achieve the butte. Up here the heat was blistering, and there was little shade to protect them from the sun. Across the canyon and a little above them they presently saw the figures of the other party.

After that they settled down to wait. Lugan, who had not spoken once this whole day, sought out the shade of a small boulder and dozed. The others laid out their ammunition, then gossiped idly. As the afternoon grew Tim became more and more uneasy. The first of Sands' herds should be in the canyon now—if he was making the drive at all. The thought that he might have guessed wrong, that Sands was even now driving the small band of cattlemen away from the Wagon Tongue, kept floating to the top of his mind. Occasionally Lugan would look at him and smile crookedly, as if to say, "Here we are. Where are your sheep?"

The sun had heeled far over when Tim suddenly jerked erect and listened. Again it came, a kind of murmur that barely pierced the hot silence of the afternoon. But it was the noise of sheep, a mass of jogging, blatting sheep already made restless by thirst. They were far from sight now, but each man took his position along the top of the butte, ready. Even Lugan, aroused at last by the excitement, came over and took his gun and bellied down, waiting.

It was fifteen minutes before a living thing showed itself on the canyon floor, and that was a jack rabbit. It scuttled down the canyon in great, lazy leaps, a warning of what was coming.

And then two horsemen came into view around the bend. Tim lined his sights and squeezed the trigger, and one of the horses went down, pitching its rider into the sand. A second shot from the other side of the canyon left the other rider without a mount. These were the opening shots, intended to turn Sands' riders back. But the two men grabbed their carbines from the saddle boot and made a dive for a projecting jut of rock. The ranchers on the west wall started to harry them, and the dismounted riders returned the fire.

Old Jeff, watching it for a moment, grunted and took aim. From his position he could see a patch of shirt showing between a crack in the rocks. He shot once, and the shirt did not move. Five seconds later one man broke loose and ran back up the canyon floor, shots from the butte kicking up geysers of sand on all sides of him. He left the other man there.

The blatting of the sheep was stronger now, but they were not yet in sight. Tim knew that the man afoot had run back to take counsel with the others.

It was fifteen minutes before the sheepmen made another move. Then from a point far down the west wall, a rifleman started throwing shots at them. He was so far away that his slugs were spent before they reached the butte. Then, down in the canyon, five men appeared on foot, running from shelter to shelter and moving toward them. It was obvious from the way these men took to cover that they had not yet discovered Tim and his crew as had the single rifleman, but believed that their path was barred only by the men on the west rock rim.

Tim held his fire and let these men work their way up the canyon. Suddenly, from down canyon on the rock rim, the warning voice of the rifleman drifted to them.

"There's two gangs!" he shouted. "Get back!"

One of the men on the canyon floor heard him. He called something to his mates, and they all looked toward the butte. Then, as they understood they were in plain sight of Tim and his crew, their courage broke. To a man, they rose and started to run back for the bend. The chorus of rifle fire from both rock rims set the afternoon throbbing with clamor. When it was over only one of the five raiders was not lying face down on the canyon floor.

And all the time, the chorus of blatting was raising its din beyond the bend. The next wait was for more than half an hour, during which the sheep kept up their forlorn protest.

"They'll try to rush it," Tim said. "It's the only move they have left."

The words were scarcely out of his mouth before the first dozen sheep poked tentative noses around the bend. No shots came to disturb them, for the ranchers on the west were taking their cue from Tim.

But Tim was curious. He motioned to hold fire, and watched what was going on down in the canyon. The sheep at the rear were being pushed hard, but the leaders were cautious. When they caught the smell of blood from the downed riders, they stopped, and in a sudden panic turned and tried to go back.

It was then that Tim signaled to open fire into them. The panic became a rout. The din that was raised brought a hot feeling of shame and anger to Tim's throat, shame that the killing of these sheep was necessary, and anger that they were being pushed blindly and cruelly into certain death.

A small band of sheep, hardier than their mates, or else more bewildered, broke and started to run ahead. Slowly and surely they were picked off by the riflemen. By now the band was in a turmoil. Hazed savagely by the invisible riders around the bend and exposed to a wild danger in the open that they could not understand, they did not know which way to turn.

But the smell of blood and the sight of the dying was stronger than fear, and they turned. They stampeded back around the bend, completely out of control, and ranchers on the butte could hear the shots being fired at them by their herders in an effort to stem the stampede.

After that it settled down to comparative quiet. The canyon floor was piled high with carcasses, and Tim spent many shells in putting the wounded ones out of their misery.

But what remained of the sheep, nevertheless, was being held beyond the bend. As the early evening wore on, the noise of their blatting increased.

"More of 'em has come!" Jeff said, smiling grimly.

"They're pilin' up in that canyon till I'll bet a man can't ride through 'em."

Once, above that din, there came down wind the sound of rifle fire from the east. It told them that the men holding the east trail were stemming the tide, too.

The sound of the thirsty and frantic sheep was beginning to anger Will Mersey. "Why the hell don't they give up?" he asked savagely. "They aim to keep these woollies here until they die?"

It seemed they did, for the din was increasing. Tim's nerves were taut with waiting. Sands was bound to try another attempt, and this time it would be with his men, rather than with the sheep. For it would be impossible to move a herd of sheep through those piles of dead down there in the canyon floor. If Sands was to come through he must first drive out the ranchers and then clear the canyon of the dead sheep.

It was almost dusk when the rifle shot cracked out above the bawling of the sheep. A slug chipped the rock by Tim's head, and he ducked down, swearing. Then began the search for the cached rifleman. At last Jeff Hardy spotted him. He was to the east, on the highest ridge in sight, but still far below them. Turning all six guns on that target, they fired a round at the ridge. Afterward the rifleman replied. But since he could not reach them if they kept away from the rim, Tim decided to ignore him.

The crew on the west rock rim were having the same trouble, and they met it the same way. For with this type of fighting the man who had eminence was bound to succeed— and the ranchers had the highest points of land within rifle-shot.

Dusk came and then darkness and still no sign of an attack. The din from the thirsty sheep had never ceased, not even with darkness.

After talking it over with Jeff, Tim decided that they were almost certain to move forward under cover of darkness. The movement in the dim depths of the canyon below attested to some activity, but it was too dark to see what was going on.

It made Tim uneasy. If the ranchers could use dynamite why couldn't the sheepmen? Well-placed shots of dynamite, planted under cover of darkness, could dislodge the ranchers by starting a slide which would bring them down in a murderous avalanche of rock. The more he thought of it, the more he worried.

Finally he said to Jeff, "Give me both your six guns. I'm goin' down."

Jeff must have been thinking the same thing, for he readily agreed. With his own two guns and Jeff's two rammed in his waistband, Tim left the butte and started working his way down the canyon wall. The footing was treacherous and he had to work carefully. The low moon put this side of the canyon in darkness, so that he could not be seen.

Hand over hand, he made his way down to the canyon floor, pausing now and then to listen and to look. Slowly his eyes got accustomed to the darkness, and he could see men working in the canyon. They were horsemen, he could see, and he thought they were dragging the sheep carcasses away. As he descended stealthily he was sure of it. They were hauling the carcasses to each side of the canyon under the cut bank, and then caving the clay overhang down on them. It was an effective way of clearing away the one barrier which would stop the sheep.

As soon as he was certain, he started to climb again. But he had not climbed ten feet before he was without any handholds. He had forgotten the way he had come down. Now he was left to grope in the dark by the trial-and-error method, and each precious moment he wasted meant that the sheep would come that much sooner. He could not call, for the riders would come over and pick him off the wall with ease!

And he could not go up!

He waited, hoping against hope that Jeff would be able to

guess at what the sheepmen were doing and make the others ready. The activity went on in that pitchy gloom, whatever noise it made being covered up by the din of the thirsty sheep around the bend.

Suddenly Tim saw the riders disappear, and he knew that it was only a matter of seconds before the sheep would be pushed through.

Taking a wild chance, he yelled, "Jeff, here they come!" and dodged across the canyon. At the same moment the blatting of the sheep grew louder, and Tim knew they were being poured into the canyon.

He ran forward, oblivious to the danger from his guns above, and started shooting at the sound of the approaching sheep.

Feet planted wide to catch the rush of these crazed animals in case they stampeded into him, he emptied one gun into the surging wave that he could not wholly see. A gun from the bend answered him, and Tim felt the whip of the slugs as they missed him. He emptied another gun at the flash of orange fire, and heard a man scream above the din of the sheep. And then he rushed forward, both guns blazing, firing blindly into the woolly torrent that was coming at him.

And belatedly, Jeff's guns from up on the cliff took up the chorus. Tim's gun flashes, seen from the butte, marked his position. Jeff was shooting ahead of him, and once more the panicked sheep began to pile up in mounds under the rain of slugs.

And once more they began to balk, and then turn, the leaders trampling the others in a desperate effort to escape from death.

And then, Tim saw a dark shape riding through the sheep, trampling them. He scarcely had time to begin shucking out the empties in his gun before the horseman bore down on him.

Tim wheeled aside, falling on his face, just as a six gun blasted loose almost at his head. The rider pulled up his horse in a rear, and, silhouetted against the sky, made a grab for his other gun.

Tim lunged at him in a long drive as his horse came down on all four feet. He heard the man grunt at the impact, and then he slipped out of the saddle, Tim clinging to him and being dragged over the hulk as they fell.

They landed in a tangle, and Tim slugged wildly in the dark. His fist caved in a derby hat, he remembered later. His second blow landed on a wide and beefy face, and then a kind of cold fury seemed to possess him.

While Jeff and his men kept pouring down a curtain of fire over them, these two fought. Muller—for it was he, wild with fury at the destruction of his sheep—fought to his feet, and stood toe to toe with Tim. There was no thought of guns, for Tim's were empty and Muller was too furious to think of his. While the sheep milled and fought not a dozen yards away from them, threatening in their panic to pour over them like a mill race let loose, they slugged at each other. There was no science about it, not even sight. They swung at each other blindly in great murdering arcs, and when one of them landed a blow the only sign was a savage grunt from the other. Toe to toe, heads lowered, oblivious to everything, the two of them slugged. It was Tim's fist, directed by some strange fortune, which caught Muller behind the ear. The thick German, dazed and angry, staggered a little and Tim was on him. He hit him three times in the face before he sprawled on his back, and then, weaving with exhaustion, Tim stood over him and waited for him to rise. But Muller was out.

The tide of the sheep, he noticed suddenly, had turned. Their blatting pandemonium had drawn away, and he was alone here in the silence.

Groggily then, he made his way down the canyon, crossed a ridge, found the horses, took his bearing and started the climb back to the butte. When he had achieved it Jeff grabbed him by the shoulder and shook him.

"Listen, boy! Listen!"

Tim listened. There was nothing to listen to, except the faint blatting of the sheep. And then it dawned on him. They were going! Sands was retreating.

"Thirty miles to water with every woolly staggering with thirst," Jeff said quietly. "I think he's licked."

Dawn found them almost through the badlands, for they were following the sheep, making sure. Even before daylight they came across sheep who were down, never to rise again.

At full daylight they were through the badlands, and they cut over to the Circle P line. Weary, grimy riders kept drifting in to the creek where their camp was. Already the men who defended the east trail were here with the news that the fight there had been bitter. But not more than a hundred sheep had got past them before Sands' men, seeing the uselessness of the fight, turned back and started the long march back to the river.

All that morning riders kept drifting in with news. Straggling bands of sheep were making their slow way through Keith's upper range to the river, hazed by cursing, raging riders. And each mile they traveled more sheep went down. Not a lamb was left. Only the toughest rams were standing the drive. As far as the eye could reach on that stretch of Keith's land there were dead and dying sheep. The hot morning sun was finishing them. The crew who had defended the west trail came in last. The fight there had been more tenacious, bitterer, but not one sheep had got through. They, too, reported that their trail coming out was thick with dead and dying sheep.

The explanation of Will Mersey's appearance and the reason for the ruse only made these men laugh now. Tim expected anger and there was none. The excitement of the day did not allow for it. Their spirits were momentarily dampened when Bennett's crew, who had helped guard the east pass, came in with the news that they had lost a man. A lucky shot had got him, but even then not one of Sands' sheep got through.

Tim left instructions that only a skeleton crew was to remain on the Circle P boundary, then got his horse and rode out alone.

11

Now that it was finished, Tim felt a little sick at the thought of what they had done. Irresistibly, he was drawn over to Keith's range. There, the sight he saw took the heart out of him. Sands' retreat to the river would be marked for years with the skeletons of these sheep. They dotted the slopes, clustered in the swales and lay along the ridges, mute and cruel evidence of one man's greed.

It was the savage and heedless waste of life that sickened Tim, and he turned away from the sight of it and rode for the Circle P. Riding into the yard he saw Martha's pony standing hipshot in the shade by the main house. His impulse was to avoid her, and he put spurs to his horse. But he was too late. Martha stepped out onto the porch to wave to him, and Tim pulled his horse over.

Martha's face was not exultant, and Tim would never forget that. She looked at him and understood a little of what he was thinking.

"I know," she said. "You've been over to see it, haven't you?"

Tim nodded.

"A week ago," Martha said pensively, "I was wishing all the sheep in the world were dead. Now I wish—I wish it didn't have to happen this way, Tim!"

"It's done now."

"And you're blaming yourself."

Tim looked down at his hands. "It was my idea," he said tonelessly.

Martha came over to him and laid a hand on his. "I've thought of that, Tim. But sometimes a man has to choose between two terrible things, doesn't he? Would you feel any better if those sheep were alive—and on Mahony's grass? Would you feel any better if they were eating away the very life of this Basin and our people were watching the work of a lifetime go to feed them?"

Tim shook his head. "No. But there must have been some other way to whip Sands."

"Tim, look at me," Martha said. Tim did. Her deep brown eyes held his for long seconds. "How long has it been since you slept?"

"I don't know," Tim answered wearily.

"It's about time you did," she said. "When you've done that maybe you'll look at it the only way we can look at it. Because we really didn't do it, Tim—it was Sands. Can't you see?"

"I reckon."

"Now go on down to the bunkhouse and sleep."

Tim did. When he turned in it was daylight and when he awakened it was daylight. He found that he almost slept the clock around. Joe Manship stomped into the bunkhouse while Tim was pulling on his boots and told him the news.

Sands had reached the river with a small band of sheep, only a fraction of his original holding. He had taken over Wiley's shack again, and things were almighty quiet in his camp. His riders were not out. But, Joe said, there was no sign that he was leaving. His men still held the bridge, which indicated that he wanted the way open for more sheep to come in. There was a small crew of cattlemen down on the line, but the bulk of the ranchers had drifted back to their places for sleep and to wait for news of Sands' next move. The nesters were still here, ready for any emergency.

Tim still felt weary as he went into the cookshack and dunned the cook for some breakfast. In spite of what

Martha had said he kept thinking of those thousands of dead sheep—dead because of his scheme and his work.

Afterward, he went out to the corral, saddled up and headed for the Ox-Bow. He wanted to hear Martha talk; he wanted to listen to old Jeff Hardy, sane and sensible.

When he rode into the Ox-Bow, Jeff was pottering around the blacksmith shop out by the wagon shed. He looked shrewdly at Tim and then talked of anything but the fight at the badlands.

"Where's Martha?" Tim asked presently.

"Ridin'."

"Alone?"

"No." Jeff gave the piece of iron in the vice a couple of swipes with the file and said without looking up, "John Lugan is ridin' with her."

Tim said nothing, but he couldn't help but feel a little anger at the news. Martha, of course, had a right to the company she chose, but it galled him to think of her choosing Lugan.

Jeff said idly, "He got pretty mouthy about your part in this ruckus. I think Martha went with him to straighten him out about some things."

"Like what?"

"He's all for us county commissioners callin' a meetin' to decide when the election for sheriff will take place."

"Isn't he satisfied with Mersey?"

Jeff spat. "No, you see he wants to run for sheriff hisself." Jeff looked up. "He figures that's the only way you can be brought to justice and put in your place, son."

Tim laughed, and Jeff laughed with him, and suddenly he was feeling better. He took some interest in what Jeff was doing then, and helped him.

An hour or so had passed and they were still at work in the blacksmith shop when Jeff walked to the door to dump his cud of tobacco. Tim heard him grunt and looked up.

There, afoot, coming down the ridge toward the corral,

was John Lugan. Jeff looked at him a moment, then hallooed. Lugan changed his course and walked toward them.

"You rode out of here with Martha, didn't you?" Jeff asked, when Lugan came up to them. His face was red with exertion, and the back of his shirt was dripping wet with sweat. He sat down and leaned his back against the shed.

"Did you ever try to ride with your cinches cut and no bridle?" he asked sourly.

"Cinches cut? Who cut 'em?"

Lugan sighed and looked up at Jeff. "There ought to be a nice way of tellin' you this, Jeff, but I don't know what it is. All I can tell you is the truth." He paused. "When we rode out of here this mornin', Charlie fixed us up a lunch. Martha wanted to ride up toward Ute Canyon, so that's what we did. We ate lunch there on the rim, and then because I hadn't had much sleep I couldn't hold out. I went to sleep. When I woke up she wasn't there and I started to look for her. First thing I noticed was that her horse was missin'. I——"

"You damn fool!" Tim said hotly. "You mean you let somebody take her!"

"Take it easy," Lugan said bluntly. "Let me finish. When I noticed the horse gone I thought that, too. I went to get my pony to look for tracks—and his bridle was gone. Besides that, the cinches were cut and my rope was gone, so I couldn't make a hackamore. I reckoned whoever got Martha did that so I couldn't follow. But I took time to look for tracks." He paused and looked at Jeff. "There wasn't any."

"No tracks? Nobody was there?"

"Not a soul. There was the tracks of Martha's pony headin' south, and that was all."

For a long moment nobody spoke, and Jeff looked up at Tim, then back at Lugan. "Meanin' she took your bridle and rope and cut your cinches?"

"I can't figure anything else, can you?" Lugan countered.

"Why would she?" Jeff asked.

"You got me there," Lugan said frankly.

Tim knelt by Lugan and balled his shirt up in his fist and yanked him erect. "Damn you, Lugan! What's happened to her?"

Lugan wasn't even angry. He looked levelly at Tim and said, "I don't know. And that's the truth."

Tim let go his shirt and said, "Get a horse! I want to see this place!"

The three of them saddled up and rode over to the lip of Ute Canyon. Lugan's pony was grazing down the slope, and Lugan caught him up.

"I suppose that damn horse has tromped the ground so we can't see a track," Tim said suspiciously.

"I done all I could," Lugan replied. "I knew you'd want to see the ground, so I drove him off down the slope. He's come back."

There, on the rim of the canyon, Jeff and Tim dismounted, and Lugan pointed out the place where he had slept and the place where the horses were. He was very thorough until Jeff said, "Shut up. I can read my own tracks."

After that, Lugan stood aside and let Jeff and Tim work the ground over. When they were finished they came back to the horses.

"Well?" Lugan asked.

"It holds water," Jeff said briefly. "It's her horse, all right. I know the tracks. Nobody else was here." He looked over at Tim. "It looks like she just picked up and left."

"For where?" Tim asked.

"I dunno. Let's see if we can track her." Jeff shook his head slowly. "If she don't want to be followed, though, we won't find a thing. She can hide sign better than an Indian."

The tracks led down the slope through the trees to the first creek, where they disappeared. Jeff took the upstream side, Tim the downstream. At dark, when they met again, neither had seen a sign of where the horse left water.

Jeff said briefly at their meeting, "There's just one thing

left to do. Make the rounds of the spreads and town and see if she's anywhere around." He divided up the territory, designated the Circle P as the meeting place and they separated.

Tim had the least likely places to touch. Bennett's, the Rutherfords', whom Martha occasionally visited, and Morgan Tanks.

At Bennett's two punchers offered to join the hunt. At Morgan Tanks the hotel was searched and every possible friend of Martha Kincaid was roused from sleep. The answers were invariable. Nobody had seen her.

In midmorning next day Tim and the two Bennett punchers rode into the Circle P. Both Lugan and Jeff were there, and so were most of the other ranchers. When Tim heard that neither Jeff nor Lugan had any trace of her, his heart sank.

He called Jeff aside and said, "Is Lugan lyin', Jeff?"

"I don't see how he can be," Jeff said. "His story fits the tracks."

"Then where can she be?"

Jeff hesitated a little before he said, "Lugan might have said somethin' threatenin' about you, and Martha left him afoot so's to ride and warn you. Then, maybe some of Sands' riders saw her and reckoned it was a chance to even scores."

Tim's face paled a little under its tan. "I'm ridin' for Sands."

"You can't," Jeff said briefly. "He'll gun you sure as hell."

"I'm goin' anyway," Tim said, turning on his heel.

Jeff headed for the bunkhouse. In another minute there were fifteen riders alongside of Tim, and this cavalcade headed straight for Wiley's place.

It was afternoon when they sloped down the bluff in plain sight of Wiley's place. A guard at the door of the shack, seeing them, gave an alarm call, and seconds later the first rifle cracked out in the afternoon silence, warning them away. There must have been fifteen ponies in the corral behind Wiley's, arguing that most of Sands' men were here.

Jeff tied a handkerchief on the end of his carbine barrel and rode ahead of the ranchers a ways. He stopped and waved it, and the shooting ceased. Presently, a group of Sands' riders clustered out in the yard. A minute passed before two horses were brought around to the front of the shack. Sands and another rider mounted.

Tim spurred on beside Jeff, and together they rode slowly toward Sands, who was approaching at about the same pace.

Sands looked haggard as he pulled up his horse and waited for them, his gunmen beside him.

Tim reined in and Jeff pulled up alongside. Five paces separated them.

"Martha Kincaid," Tim said quietly, "can't be found, Sands. Did you kidnap her?" There was a quiet menace in his voice that worried Jeff. He was wondering what would happen if Tim lost his temper.

"She didn't tell you?" Sands asked, then added thoughtfully, "No, I don't suppose she would."

"Tell us what?" Tim said swiftly.

"Miss Kincaid has left the country," Sands said calmly. "I was wakened a little after midnight last night by one of my crew. I dressed and went out, and Miss Kincaid was waiting to talk to me. She informed me that she was leaving the country."

"You're a liar!" Tim said hotly. Swiftly, Jeff laid a hand on his arm.

Sands stroked his mustache with his thumb, his eyes speculative and polite.

"Go on," Jeff said.

"And have that idiot try to blow my brains out. No, thank you," Sands said dryly. "Is that all you want?"

"He'll keep quiet," Jeff promised. "I want to hear more about her visit to you."

Sands looked undecided. Tim, however, was still as death, and Sands asked, "What else do you want to know?"

"Why did she come to you?" Jeff asked.

"I don't see any reason for telling you," Sands murmured. "I would not be believed."

"Try us."

Sands inclined his head in assent. "She informed me that she was leaving the country and wanted to know if I was still in the market for the nester places along the river. If I was, she said, she wanted to sell out."

"Were you?" Jeff asked quietly.

"I was. I paid her five thousand dollars for her place. If you'll take the trouble to notice, my men are occupying it this morning."

Tim made no movement, did not even look at Jeff. Jeff cleared his throat and said, "There's only one thing that'll prove that, Sands. Did she give you a deed?"

"I have it here in my pocket," Sands said. "In my inside coat pocket. Do you want to see it?"

"Yes."

Slowly, Sands reached in his pocket and brought out a piece of paper. Jeff pulled his horse over to take it. He looked at it carefully, then handed it back.

"Is it her writing?" Tim asked him.

"I can't tell," Jeff said. "It looks enough like it."

Sands only smiled faintly and said nothing.

"Did she give you any reason for her leavin'?" Jeff asked finally.

"Yes, I doubt if you'd believe it, though."

"Try us," Jeff said again.

"She said she was sick of fighting," Sands said quietly. "She evidently believed that after my unsuccessful try for water on Mahony's range I would give up. But she said when I came back here and it looked as if I was going to fight it out, she made up her mind to leave. I told her most certainly I was going to stay—unless I was allowed to run sheep in this Basin without molestation." He smiled meagerly. "That seemed to make up her mind for her."

"Sands," Tim said quietly, "a bigger liar than you never lived."

Sands nodded indifferently and said nothing. He obviously knew he had the upper hand, and didn't seem to care whether he was believed or not.

Tim went on, "If I thought you'd taken her, kidnapped her, I'd kill you now."

"You're entitled to think whatever you damn please," Sands drawled. "And any time you feel like trying to down me I'm ready for you. But"—and here he smiled again—"I would not like to have you try in the hopes that you will find Miss Kincaid locked in Wiley's barn. You would be disappointed."

He waited a moment and then said, "Is that all?"

"One thing more," Jeff said stubbornly. "Did she say where she was going?"

"I didn't ask," Sands replied. "She asked me if I'd mind if she took a few personal things out of her cabin. I said no." He paused. "Oh yes. She said to tell her Negro hand that he was to ask you for a job, Hardy. That's all."

"Thanks," Jeff said briefly. He pulled his horse away, but Tim just sat there, staring at the ground. "Come along, Tim," Jeff said. Tim roused himself, took one long look at Sands, and wheeled his horse.

Jeff told the ranchers what Sands had related and they headed for the Ox-Bow. Jeff wanted to say something, but the look on Tim's face checked him for a long while.

Finally Tim asked quietly, "Do you believe she'd do it, Jeff?"

"No."

Tim looked swiftly at him. "Then Sands has got her?"

"What else could have happened to her?"

Tim pulled up his horse, his mouth open to speak, but Jeff said wearily, "Hell, son, it ain't goin' to get her back for you to commit suicide. If he's got her he won't hurt her. And she's safe enough, I reckon."

"But why did he do it?" Tim asked savagely. "If he did."

Jeff patted his gun at his thigh. "You take the spring out of a six gun, son, and it don't look any different. You could

even fool a man with it. But it won't work." He shook his
head. "Martha was the spring in our six gun, Tim. Sands
was wise enough to see that. Without her to drive us, to
rawhide us, Sands figures we won't be much good. And I
reckon we won't," he added. After a long pause he said, *"If
he took her."*

12

When Martha rode into Peavey between her three guards
she was almost too tired to notice her surroundings. She had
been in the saddle almost twenty-four hours, with only occasional rests. Everything had come too fast for her, and she
was bewildered. She still did not understand it all, except
that John Lugan was a traitor.

Yesterday, when she went riding with him at his request,
she had suggested they ride up toward Ute Canyon. But he
had demurred, and to be agreeable, she submitted to his
suggestion that they circle around the Ox-Bow and head
north, and have lunch way up on the Wagon Tongue above
Bennett's B Slash. He had set a swift pace, hardly a pleasant
one, but she had gamely kept even with him. When they
reached the Wagon Tongue at the old mine site, there were
three men waiting for them. Lugan had informed her then
that she was to go with them. He wanted her horse, too, he
said.

She had refused, of course, but John Lugan only laughed.
He lifted her off her horse, put her on the other one, touched
his hat and bid her good-by. Immediately, she tried to break
away from her guards. They caught her easily, and then one
of them put the proposition to her that they wouldn't touch
her, wouldn't harm her in any way if she would come with

them. They were rough-looking men, and she already guessed they were Sands' riders. She submitted, simply because escape seemed hopeless. She was being kidnapped, but the reason for it escaped her. And she could not tell where they were taking her.

Peavey, in the noon sun, was not an inviting place. A tumble-down building by the creek, with its pile of weather-browned sawdust and rusty machinery, called the name of the town to mind. She remembered riders speaking of Peavey, although the Basin men seldom visited it. It was a stopping place for men on the dodge, a kind of shady and furtive place where men did not ask questions. Only half of its dozen shacks were lived in. The old hotel, with its barroom, was still standing in unpainted ugliness at the head of a stump-pocked street, and it was here they were taking her. All around the small brush-grown clearing of the town was the pine forest. Even in midday there was a quiet hissing of the wind through these dark trees.

A young puncher was standing on the steps of the hotel when they rode up to it. He came over and helped Martha dismount, and then said, "Come along with me, miss."

He stood aside and let her pass into the lobby. Martha stopped abruptly inside the door, and looked at the girl standing in the middle of the lobby. They looked at each other a long moment, and then the girl said, "St Cloud, who is she?"

"I'm Martha Kincaid. You're Julie Sands, aren't you?"

Julie nodded and came over to her. St Cloud by the doorway was looking uncomfortable under Julie's stare. "What's she doin' here, St Cloud?"

"Your dad's orders, Miss Julie."

"I can tell you," Martha said quietly. "I was kidnapped by your father's riders."

"Oh." Julie looked at her carefully and then shuttled her glance to St Cloud. "Is that true?"

"Yes'm," St Cloud said.

"Why?"

"I dunno. It's your dad's orders, Miss Julie. He said for you to look after her while she was here—get her clothes, and such."

Julie's lip curled in scorn and St Cloud looked away. To Martha she said, "Did they hurt you?"

"No. Only—why was it done?"

"Sheep," Julie said bitterly. "That's the answer to everything in my life. Yours, too, I guess." She shrugged. "Well, you better make the best of it. Come upstairs and we'll find you some clothes."

Martha was shown in her room by a fat, stolid-faced Indian woman. Julie brought her a dress to wear, but Martha did not put it on, preferring her jeans. She stood at the window, looking out onto the mean little shacks and the old mill shed. Tornado Basin, with its bitter war, seemed far away now. And she was helpless to share in it, no matter how much she wanted to. It was obvious enough now that Sands wanted her out of the Basin. Why? Was he preparing to wage a new kind of fight, one of bushwack and raiding and death, and wanted to be free of the responsibility of harming a woman? No, that wasn't so, for Mrs. Mahony, Ray Bennett's sister and other women remained. Then what was it? She couldn't understand any of it. Lugan was the man who had sold out to Sands; he was the man who was responsible for old Keith's death. And only Tim's sensible precaution in insisting that all the Basin riders travel in threes had kept Lugan from giving away the trap in the badlands. But what was to prevent him from betraying Tim and old Jeff in other ways—and worse ones. Martha found that her body was tense with the thinking of it, and she turned away from the window. She must get word to Tim to watch out for Lugan. But how?

There came a tap on her door and the Ute woman informed her that her meal was ready below. Downstairs, in the dining room, Julie Sands was waiting for her.

Martha sat down to her food and Julie chose a chair

across the table. Martha tried bravely to eat for she was hungry, but the food stuck in her throat.

"You're worried," Julie said abruptly.

"Wouldn't you be?"

"Not in the slightest," Julie said frankly. "You're out of an unpleasant mess."

Resentment stirred within Martha at the coolness of this dark and beautiful girl. "Yes, it's a mess," she agreed. "Unpleasant, too. Only it holds about everything I care for."

"Like what?" Julie asked curiously.

"Well, my friends, for one thing. Then I have a home there—the only place I can call home."

Julie listened gravely. "You mean you're worried about your friends?" she asked, when Martha was finished. "Can't they take care of themselves?"

"I—I guess so," Martha replied, a little surprised at the callous tone Julie was using. And then she thought of Lugan and was suddenly angry. "They could, that is, if your father hadn't bought one of the ranchers out. You see, I think he'll betray us."

"How?"

Martha shrugged. "Why—how does a traitor betray? I suppose he'll lead them into some sort of a trap, where your father can wipe them out. That's what your father wants isn't it?"

"I'm sure I don't know," Julie said idly.

Martha only looked at her strangely, and then tried again to eat the food before her. But it wouldn't work. She pushed the plate from her in a gesture of weariness. Julie watched her closely.

"You're really worried about your friends, then?" she asked.

"Terribly," Martha confessed. When she looked up Julie was smiling a little. "Is there anything amusing about that?" Martha asked resentfully. "In my place, wouldn't you feel the same?"

"I can't tell. I haven't any friends," Julie replied.

"That—why, that can't be!"

Julie nodded. "Besides," she said slowly, "I don't think it's your friends you're worried about. Isn't he more than a friend?"

"Who?"

"Tim Enever, of course."

Martha felt the color crawling into her face. She couldn't understand this girl, so callous in some ways, so sharp in others. She knew her manner betrayed her, and she did not intend to lie.

"Yes, he is. But there are others, my friends."

"I'm not talking about them. I'm talking about him," Julie said calmly. "He's the one you're worried about. Are you in love with him?"

Martha stared at her in amazement. There was no reticence in this daughter of Sands, only a kind of curiosity that was more like prying. And yet it wasn't that. She was so frank that it was disquieting. Martha thought about the question, and then she knew that she didn't have to think about it, that it had been settled in her own mind these many days past.

"Yes," she said quietly. "Now do you blame me for being worried?"

"I blame you for being a fool," Julie said calmly.

"You don't know him!" Martha flared.

"I do. I think you're a fool." She spoke calmly enough, but there was an undercurrent of passion in her tone.

"I would rather be my kind of a fool than your kind of a wise woman," Martha said hotly. She knew she was being baited, but in her anger she didn't care. "You don't know him!" she repeated stubbornly, helplessly.

"I know he's like my father," Julie said quietly.

Anger whipped into Martha's eyes. She found that she was clenching her fists until they hurt. A kind of hot loyalty to Tim welled up in her, and the mention of Sands was like the flick of a whip. "Your father," she said in a tight contemptuous voice. "If you have the courage to bring up his name, then you deserve anything I can say about him! He's a killer—a filthy, cowardly murderer who hasn't the courage to do his own lying and fighting and killing!"

"Perhaps," Julie admitted calmly. "But your Tim is the same kind."

"He's not! He's clean and loyal and fine!"

Julie leaned across the table and said quietly, "So was Dad—before he found out he could think a little faster and a little straighter and a little longer than most men. And when he found that out it did something to him. It made him want to twist and trample and break men. It does that to all men —all men."

"Not to Tim!"

"Wait," Julie said quietly. "If Dad doesn't down him in this fight then he'll down Dad. And when he's done that it will give him a taste for blood—like a sheep-killing dog." Her lip lifted a little in scorn. "He's no different than any man, your Tim. He means waiting and humiliation and heartbreak for any woman!"

Martha winced under the lash of this girl's scorn, and suddenly she pitied her. "You must have had a pretty rotten life of it, Julie, to talk that way."

Julie laughed shortly. "Rotten? Hardly. I just know men, that's all. I've lived with them all my life. They're all alike— only some are a little sharper, a little more greedy, a little quicker in anger than others. The woman who puts her trust in one is a fool! She deserves everything she gets—and more. Your Tim isn't any different. He's only like Dad—a little worse than most. And that only means misery for you."

She stood up, moved by her own passionate speech. She walked to the window and pulled back the sleazy curtains. Martha stared at the table, silent. This girl had no power to touch her, no power to convince her.

Suddenly she felt Julie's hands on her shoulders. "I'm sorry," Julie said softly. "Only every once in a while I have to get it out of my system. What—what makes me afraid is that I believe it myself."

Martha half turned in her chair. "It isn't so," she said quietly. "I know it isn't so. You've only had rotten luck, Julie." Her eyes grew pensive. "There's old Jeff Hardy. I've known him since I was a little girl. There's nothing bad about him. He's kind and gentle and he isn't greedy. Why, every man in this Basin owes his land, his cattle, his very home to Jeff Hardy. He's sharper and quicker than other men, Julie. But he's gentler and kinder and more tolerant. If he's big in the things that make for badness in men, then he's big in the things that make for good."

"I've never known a man like that," Julie murmured. "I —I didn't know there were any."

"I know—two," Martha said softly. "Jeff and Tim."

Julie shivered a little and let her hands slip from Martha's shoulders. Without another word she left the room. Compassion and pity for her welled up in Martha, and a kind of anger, too—anger that life with a man like Sands could warp his daughter into his own cynical mold. There was a desperation in Julie that showed in her eyes, in her sulky defiant speech. If she wasn't separated from these men and from her father it wouldn't be long before she was broken. The thought of it depressed Martha, and she rose, leaving her food untouched.

Out in the lobby she looked around her. It was deserted. The right-angled counter in the corner by the stairs held no register, no pen. The rack of pigeonholes behind it was stuffed with miscellaneous gear—a pair of gloves, an odd spur, a file. The board where the keys hung was empty. Two rickety chairs leaned against the far wall, and the big front window was dirty and fly specked. It was run down and shabby, all of it, and there was a kind of weariness about its very boards that made Martha hate it.

She walked to the door and out onto the porch. The clean, still-faced puncher came to his feet. He had been sitting in the single chair, tilting back against the wall.

Martha looked at him closely, wondering at him. Beneath the kind of alert defiance in his face there was a friendliness that did not quite break through. It stopped just short of trust and liking.

"Can I go out?" she asked.

St Cloud nodded briefly. "Anywhere you want, miss—except the barn. The horses are under lock, so you'll save yourself the trouble of tryin' to break them out and ride away."

"Are you our guard?"

"Yes'm."

"Does Julie ride?"

"She did. She don't now that you're here."

"Then she's a prisoner, too?"

St Cloud almost smiled. "Looks like that, ma'am."

"Sands must be a pleasant man," Martha murmured dryly. "He treats his daughter exactly like a prisoner."

Something flickered in St Cloud's eyes, then died. He said nothing.

"How long are you going to keep me here?" Martha went on.

"As long as he says, ma'am."

"Until he's murdered his way into Tornado Basin?" Martha asked bitterly.

St Cloud shifted his eyes away from her and said nothing.

"You must be proud to work for him," Martha taunted. "Were you raised sheepman?"

"No, ma'am."

"And you turned renegade for his money?"

St Cloud's eyes flickered to her. It seemed he was about to say something, and then his slight clean-shaped face settled into stubbornness again. He looked away from her, but made no offer to leave. Martha remembered Julie's open contempt for him, and for a moment she felt a pity for him. He wasn't like the others; he seemed to have a hidden and untouchable pride behind his iron politeness.

"I'm sorry," Martha said dully. "I suppose we all have to live. And we can't always have a choice."

St Cloud's face softened a little, but he did not speak.

Martha turned back into the hotel and went upstairs to her room. She was weary and wanted to lie down, but a driving restlessness would not allow her to. She stood at the window, looking out. From her room she could look down on the bare back yard of the hotel.

While she was standing there a man left the hotel and went out to the barn. He was a great tub of a man in boots whose heels were run over, as if they could not support the great slack weight of him. He unlocked the door, brought out a horse, locked the door again, saddled up and then rode off slowly through the clearing.

The Indian woman came out after he left. She stood in the middle of the yard, looking in the direction he had gone. In the very lack of any gesture or any movement, she contrived to show her loathing for this man who had ridden out. It was as plain to Martha as if she had shouted it. Was he her husband? Martha wondered. She watched as the woman went out to the woodshed, loaded her dirty apron with short lengths of stovewood, then returned to the kitchen, her gait a broken shuffle, like that of a weary pack horse.

It was that which started Martha wondering. She knew the lot of the Indian woman who married a white man. It was usually a hard life of drudgery and loneliness, ending in a kind of sullen submission that was often threaded with hatred. Maybe, Martha thought, this Ute woman was like that.

She slipped out into the hallway and listened. There was not a sound in the hotel. Softly, she stole down the stairway, and still it was quiet. A long corridor led back past the stairs to the kitchen, and small sounds from there told Martha where the Ute woman was working.

At the kitchen door she paused and opened it stealthily. The Indian woman was alone. A dozen loaves of baked bread were laid out on the big table in the center of the room, and the warm smell of yeast pervaded the room.

Martha slipped inside and closed the door after her. The

Ute woman stood immobile, looking at her, a stick of stovewood in her hand.

Martha walked over to her, smiling. "You understand English, don't you?"

The Ute woman nodded.

"Are you allowed to leave here?" Martha asked. "Do you ever ride out?"

"I go visit family over mountains," the Ute woman said stolidly.

"For how long?"

"Four-five days sometimes."

"Doesn't your husband mind?"

Something stirred in the woman's dark eyes. "He don' stop me. I go."

Martha was satisfied. "Can you take a note for me down to the Ox-Bow ranch? You know where it is?"

The woman nodded.

"I'll pay you for it," Martha said swiftly. She suddenly remembered that she had no money with her. The only thing of value she had was the locket around her neck under her shirt—a locket of her mother's. It was gold, set with several small diamonds, and inside it was a picture of her mother and father. It made her a little sick to think of parting with it, and for one moment hesitated. The impassive eyes of the Indian woman watched her. With an almost frantic haste Martha unfastened the locket and gave it to the woman. She held it in a fat brown hand, turning it over and over, so that the small diamonds played in the dull light. To her it was only a bright and shining trinket, and Martha could see that she liked it.

"Have you a pencil?" Martha asked.

The Indian woman went out into the corridor and up to the desk. She brought back a cheap tablet and the stub of a pencil, and tendered them to Martha.

Martha wrote: "Tim, I'm at Peavey. Watch out for John Lugan. He is Sands' man. Martha."

Folding it, she gave it to the Indian woman. "When will you go?" she asked breathlessly.

The Indian did not move.

"The first chance you get?" Martha persisted.

The Indian woman nodded.

"Look," Martha said quickly. "You've got to get to the Ox-Bow with it! The lives of many men depend on it! Do you understand?"

Again the woman nodded.

"And you've got to hurry. Will you go tonight?"

The same nod again. Martha wondered if she understood. She could only hope. She wished desperately that she could tell if the woman understood the importance of it, but those brown searching eyes gave no clue to what the woman was thinking. She had turned to her fire stoking again, and Martha went out.

Upstairs, a great weariness came over her—weariness and a sense of relief, a growing of hope. She lay down and was asleep immediately.

It was dark when she was awakened by a knock at her door, and the Ute woman announced that supper was ready.

Martha went downstairs. Julie and St Cloud were both in the dining room waiting for her. Julie looked sulky and she only nodded at Martha's entrance.

They sat down. St Cloud, across the table from Martha, reached in his pocket and drew out something and reached across the table to lay it before Martha.

When he drew his hand away, Martha saw it was her locket. She stared at it for one bleak second, and then raised her glance to St Cloud's face. Behind the stubborn set of it there was a pity that Martha did not see.

"Oh," Martha said in a small voice. "You—you heard me, then."

St Cloud moved his head in negation. "It don't do any good, miss, to fight it. You can't fight it with money. Sands will double any bribe that's offered to the folks who work for him. That breed woman earned a hundred dollars by turnin' that locket over to me." He leaned over and tossed the note beside the locket.

"Maybe we better eat," he said quietly.

13

Sands looked around Martha's cabin with a critical air. If he saw the curtains, the flowers, if he noticed the clean lamp chimney, the scrubbed floor now littered with the cigarette butts of the men he had just ordered over to Wiley's, he gave no sign of it. The room was small, so that his pacing was not really pacing, but rather a kind of wandering restlessness, a moving impatience.

A man came to the door out of the night and said, "He's here, chief. I hear him."

"All right. All right," Sands said impatiently.

He drew out a cigar, slapped his pockets for a match and then went over to the lamp. He held the cigar over the chimney, sucking it into burning. A whole inch of the cigar caught fire, however, and with a savage gesture he threw it out the door.

A minute later John Lugan stepped into the room, nodded to Sands and closed the door. Lugan was angry, his nostrils dilated a little with the effort to keep his temper.

"The next time you send one of your men to get me, Sands, for God's sake be a little more private about it!"

"Then keep in touch with me more often," Sands countered curtly.

"I come here when I have something to tell you!" Lugan retorted, his voice rising a little. "I'm not going to get myself shot just because you happen to want to ask me questions!"

They stood there in that small room, about ten feet apart, glaring at each other.

"Just what happened?" Sands asked.

"Your man came up to my place and asked the cook where I was."

"I don't see where that's dangerous."

"I'll tell you. My cook doesn't happen to be deaf and dumb. He's apt to talk to the crew, and they're apt to talk to other crews."

"Nonsense!" Sands said curtly. "How do you expect me to find you if my men don't ask your whereabouts? When I want you I want you right now, not when it's handy for you to come." He added sharply, "You understand?"

Lugan nodded. "Yeah, I understand," he said grimly. "Just the same I'm goin' to take a gun to the next rider of yours that doesn't use some care."

Sands took a step toward him. "You're going to what?" he asked mildly.

"You heard me!" Lugan said hotly. "I've got too much at stake to risk bein' given away by one of your blunderin' gunnies!"

Sands was breathing hard now. He waited a long moment before he answered softly, "Let's settle who's running this business right now, Lugan. Am I, or are you?"

"You are."

"Correct. I give the orders?"

"Yes."

"Suppose I give one now, then," Sands said. His voice was trembling a little with anger. "I repeat, you're here at my convenience—always. The next time you aren't I believe a note to Tim Enever will settle the question, and settle it for good." His eyes narrowed. "You've made the mistake, Lugan, of thinking you're too valuable to me. You aren't."

"I've done what I could," Lugan said stubbornly.

"Which isn't enough. For one thing I would have had several thousand more sheep at the present moment if you'd been on your toes."

"You planned that drive without even tellin' me!"

"I had to. On the other hand, you let that drive come off without warning me what I was in for."

"I couldn't get away, I told you!"

"It's your business to get away," Sands said implacably. "From now on, you will get away—or I'm through with you. I don't see the wisdom of paying a spy when he can't get information to me."

"I did the best I could."

"It isn't good enough!" Sands said vehemently. "I'm warning you, Lugan, another slip like that and I'll turn you over to your rancher friends with evidence enough to hang you so high the birds can't get at you!"

All the truculence seemed to have left Lugan. He licked his lips and sat down, avoiding Sands' eye. "All right. Only I can't do better than my best. What do you want with me?"

"What's happening over there since the girl's gone?"

"It didn't work," Lugan said flatly. "They don't believe you."

"Not the forgery?"

"They believe that, yes. But they don't believe she'd leave them."

"The fools!" Sands said. "They can't believe both. If they think the deed is genuine how can they help but believe she's left?"

"I'm not tryin' to explain. I'm just tellin' you what happened."

Sands turned on his heel and started his aimless pacing again. "What did you do?" he said over his shoulder.

"I damn near got my head knocked by Enever," Lugan growled. "I come right out and said it looked like she'd run out on us. It took two men to haul him off me."

Sands smiled briefly. "I gave him credit for being a realist, anyway. It seems I'm wrong."

"He believes you've got her. He isn't sure, and neither is old Hardy. If they were you'd have them swarmin' all over you, Sands. But they don't know what to think—except that she didn't run away. The rest of them don't think. They haven't even got an idea."

Sands pondered this a while, looking absently out the window. "Enever doesn't intend to pull out after that?"

It was Lugan's turn to laugh. "Pull out? You couldn't get him out of the county with a twenty-mule team."

Sands looked over at Lugan, regarding him sharply, then looked away. He didn't speak for a full minute. Suddenly he straightened up and came over to face Lugan.

"I've wanted to avoid this, but I can't any longer. I don't like the idea of bringing a swarm of Cattle Association men down on my head. But I've got to risk it." He paused. "Enever has got to be killed."

"I could have told you that long ago," Lugan said.

Sands ignored that. He said quietly, "How are you going to do it, Lugan?"

Lugan at first didn't get the significance of the question. He scowled at the floor, and then, thought quick, his glance yanked up to Sands' face.

"Me?"

"That's what I said."

Lugan stood up. "I won't touch it, Sands! I thought that was the agreement to begin with!"

"It was. It's changed."

"I won't do it!" Lugan said stubbornly.

"You will. You'll do it or I'll turn you over to your friends."

"But you gave your word!"

Sands nodded. "I thought it would come to this. It has—word or no word. You'll kill him."

Lugan was sweating. He looked helplessly about the room, and then sat down again, folding his hands because they were trembling. He was afraid, and it showed in every line of his face. Sands watched him with a quiet smile of contempt raising his mustaches.

"How?" Lugan said huskily.

"That's up to you."

"But I can't beef him!" Lugan said. "He never travels alone! He's quick as a cat and suspicious as hell!"

"You'll do it," Sands murmured. "You can do anything when you *have* to," he added meaningly.

Lugan rubbed his face with both hands. "How much time have I got?" he asked.

Sands sat down on the chair next to the table. "Tonight," he said, "I'm leaving for Rincon, over south. I'm wiring to my man over the mountains here. In two days I'll have three big bands starting up the east side of the Tornadoes way above the Ox-Bow. Before they reach the pass up there I'll have twenty additional men here. After that I'm going to raid. I'm going to wipe this valley clean, so that when my sheep have come down this side of the Tornadoes there won't be a cattleman to bother them." He paused. "These men of mine should be here in a week. By that time I want Enever out of the way."

"A week then?"

"About." He stood up. "In case you think you can double-cross me, Lugan, and lead these ranchers against my men while I'm gone, I'll put your mind at rest. When I go my men will scatter to the mountains and wait for my return."

"What about your sheep?"

"Hell with them," Sands said. "Let them forage for themselves. There aren't enough left to bother with."

Lugan stood up now. "You're a hard man, Sands. When I agreed to come in with you I didn't know I was joinin' up with a man who wouldn't stick at murder—any murder."

"When you own your third of the Basin you'll forget that."

"When I do, maybe I will," Lugan agreed. "Only, what you're aimin' to do will pull a U.S. marshal down here, sure as rain. And what you're crowdin' me into doin' will pull the Cattle Association men in here, too."

"I've fought both before," Sands said quietly. "Licked them, too." He made an impatient gesture. "I'm tired of waiting. With Enever out of the way, I'll take his Basin in a week."

Lugan said nothing. He turned and put his hand on the door latch.

"A week, remember," Sands reminded him.

Lugan didn't seem to hear. He was studying the older man with quiet intent. "All right," he said placidly. "But I'll tell you one thing, Sands. If I ever see the chance to double-cross you and still save my hide I'll do it so fast it will sound like the wind in the trees."

Sands nodded. "Of course."

"Good night."

"Good night."

14

Once safely past the Circle P boundary, which was still being patrolled by patient riders, Lugan gave his horse its head and reviewed the night's conversation. He was past anger; in its place was a desperate urgency. He had to do something and do it quickly. He thought of the possibility of circling back and making a try for Sands on the road to Rincon. But he knew he wouldn't succeed. Sands never traveled without four gunmen. Even if he downed him, he himself would be hunted down and killed. That was out. There was the alternative of betraying Sands' plans to Jeff Hardy and casting himself on Jeff's mercy. That, he understood, would be the equivalent of suicide. Jeff might try to save him, but the others would get him. Nor could he betray Sands anonymously, for Sands would know the source of his betrayal and act accordingly.

No, there was one thing left to do, and that was Sands'

bidding. He would have to kill Tim Enever. Every move in this game of Sands' was as logical as time, as irrevocable as death. Sands made no mistakes, only waited for other men to make them. Lugan could remember the one other time when he tried to double-cross Sands. That was when he had tried to persuade Borden that night in the hotel room at their secret meeting that both of them should murder Sands and seize his sheep. But Sheriff Borden at bottom was an honest man, and Lugan had had to kill him to keep him from going to Sands and to the ranchers. Sands was lucky, that was all. And you couldn't beat luck when it was teamed with brains. And slowly but surely Sands was cornering him now. He lured a man with money, enmeshed him with the violence of his own deeds, and discarded him when he was through with him. Sands hadn't discarded him yet, but he would. And still there was no way out, nothing to do except fight bitterly for survival.

He turned his thoughts to the murder of Tim Enever. His mind, for good, was made up. Tim Enever couldn't be killed by simple shooting. In the first place, he was riding these hills in the hunt for Martha Kincaid. In the second place, he was suspicious of Lugan. In the third place, he hunted with that old wolf of a Jeff Hardy. Open bushwhack was out of the question.

Then what was left? A trap—a trap that he would walk into alone and eagerly. Lugan turned that over in his mind for a long time, choosing, discarding. Suddenly it occurred to him, and with such violence that he yanked his horse to a stop. Unconsciously he turned his head toward the Tornadoes, and looked at them. Of course.

He set out toward the foothills at a long lope. Later, when he was in the timber, his pace was slowed a little, but it was steady enough as he picked his way up the slope toward Peavey.

At midday he rode into the town. That morning a slow drizzle had set in, and toward midday it was rushed on a raw wind into his face. He arrived at Peavey weary and wet under his slicker, and hungry, his mood savage.

St Cloud tilted back in his chair on the hotel porch, saw him enter the weed-grown street and head for the hotel. Unconsciously St Cloud shifted his holster to a position where he could easily reach it.

When Lugan was close enough for St Cloud to recognize him, St Cloud let his chair down and stood up, breathing a little easier.

"Howdy," St Cloud said.

"Howdy. Martha Kincaid in her room?" Lugan asked.

"She's eatin' with Miss Julie in the dinin' room."

"Her room locked?"

"No. Why?"

"I want somethin' there," Lugan said. "Come along with me and show me, will you?"

St Cloud hesitated. He had the average man's wholesome dislike for a traitor, and he knew Lugan to be one. But, on the other hand, Sands treated him as a business partner, and St Cloud took his cue from that. He led the way upstairs and into Martha's room.

Lugan looked around the room, which was clean and neat. "She got any clothes?" he asked.

"She's wearin' Miss Julie's."

"What about the ones she took off?"

St Cloud shrugged. Lugan walked over to the rickety bureau and wrestled impatiently with one of the drawers. It shot open with sudden violence, slipped out of his hands and clattered to the floor.

Martha's clean shirt and jeans and neckerchief tumbled out onto the floor. It was a black silk neckerchief and it was knotted around a thick silver ring with an inset of pale and excellent turquoise. It was a curious ring, and Lugan remembered that Martha almost always wore it with the neckerchief. He picked up the ring and the neckerchief and rammed them in his pocket.

"What's that for?" St Cloud asked.

"Bait," Lugan said enigmatically. "If she misses this don't tell her where it is."

St Cloud said nothing, his eyes watchful and deeply suspicious.

"I want food," Lugan said.

"You can go down and eat with Miss Kincaid," St Cloud said dryly. "She talks about you a lot."

Lugan flushed. "Watch your lip, cowboy," he said sharply. "I want food."

"There's a side of mutton downstairs," St Cloud murmured. "You'd better start gettin' used to it."

"Damn you!" Lugan said, taking a step toward him. "You'd better close your mouth before I close it for you!"

St Cloud smiled crookedly. His eyes were scornful, cold, insolent. He did not move, did not even indicate that Lugan's threat impressed him. Lazily, he lounged erect.

"Boo!" he said, and laughed softly, then went out.

Later, after Lugan had snatched a hasty meal in the kitchen and mounted again, he saw St Cloud lounging against the porch pillar watching him. It didn't matter if this tough kid did tell Martha he'd been there. All he'd wanted was to avoid seeing her.

His camp that night was almost in the foothills, and it was a miserable one. He only paused to rest his horse. Without blankets or food, and with only a sputtering fire to keep him company during the long night, he waited impatiently for dawn.

The rain ceased before daylight and the day broke clear. He rode steadily for the Circle P, and once within its boundaries, he checked his pace and tried to recall the camps of the men patrolling the boundary. There was one on the Wagon Tongue, he remembered, a nester one, and he turned south, heading for it.

The camp was little more than a half-dozen bedrolls under a big cottonwood, and when Lugan rode into it he was pleased to see that somebody was making fire and preparing a breakfast.

To Lugan's quiet satisfaction, there were only two nesters in camp. They were rustling up breakfast preparatory to riding out to relieve the patrol. He remembered that the name of one of them was Kelso, a cousin of Wiley's. He was a slight man, past middle age and he moved with the spare motions of a man who knows rheumatism. His clothes were threadbare and dirty, and his unshaven face was set in a kind of sullen resentment. Ray Bennett had once thrashed him with a rope end when he caught him over a branding fire with a B Slash calf at the end of his rope. His place was small, Lugan remembered, with a sod shack for a house. Most of his land was bog, so useless that Sands had refused to consider buying it. His loyalty to the ranchers was inspired by resentment at Sands more than anything else, Lugan suspected.

Kelso's partner was younger. Lugan remembered him as a swamper in the Gem, until George Moriarty fired him for stealing liquor. If Lugan had combed the ranks of most disgruntled and disreputable nesters, he could not have found two men more suited to his purpose.

He nodded curtly as he dismounted, and said, "Any grub?"

"Help yourself," Kelso said, indicating some cold pan bread and steaks.

Lugan was ravenous, but when he looked at the food he made a wry face.

"Hell, hasn't Enever given you anything besides this muck?" he asked.

Kelso glanced obliquely at his partner, as if he were looking to see if he understood Lugan. His companion gave him no help, and he switched his attention back again to Lugan, who was rolling a smoke. "You talk like we was losin' this fight against Sands instead of winnin' it, Lugan."

"Sands?" Lugan echoed. "Who's talkin' about Sands? He's taken care of. I'm talkin' about losin' to Enever—and Jeff Hardy."

"Losin' what?"

Lugan looked at him pityingly. "Why your land, you damn fool," he said calmly.

"They don't want my land," Kelso said. "They're helpin' me to keep it, ain't they?"

"To keep it from Sands, yes. But they'll get it themselves."

"Jeff Hardy and Tim Enever?" Kelso laughed. "What would they want with it?"

"What do they want with all that strip you nesters own? What did they want with Keith's that they killed him for it?" He paused. "They just want all the Basin, that's all."

Kelso's eyes narrowed. "Keith? Did you say they killed Keith?"

"I did. There never was any fight with Sands' men there at Keith's. Did anybody see the bodies of those four men they were supposed to kill?"

"Pete Turner."

Lugan came over and squatted by Kelso. "Listen," he said quietly. "If you were the witness to a murder and tried to run away and got shot twice in the leg, so you couldn't run away, and there were two men there holdin' a gun to your head, wouldn't you promise to keep your mouth shut? Wouldn't you lie when somebody asked you about that murder—especially if you was promised a job as foreman of a big spread."

"Was Turner promised a job?"

"As Enever's foreman, when they get this Basin. Same as Will Mersey."

"What about him?" Kelso asked slowly.

"Why, he's goin' to be Jeff Hardy's foreman," Lugan said calmly. "What do you suppose?"

Kelso stared at him for a long moment. "How do you figure that?"

"Why don't Mersey arrest Enever for Borden's murder?" Lugan countered.

Kelso thought this over a moment. "Why, Miss Kincaid said it was because Enever never done it."

"And where is Miss Kincaid now?"

"Gone."

"Run away, you mean," Lugan said. "She found out about it. She's the one who told me about it before she left. It was a little too strong for her stomach."

Kelso scowled. "Wait a minute," he said. "I don't get all this. Jeff Hardy and Tim Enever aim to take over this Basin, along with Pete Turner and Will Mersey, and Miss Kincaid found out about it and pulled out."

Lugan nodded. "After she saw that deal they pulled on Mersey."

"What was that?" Kelso's crafty face was alert now, intent.

"Why, everyone knows now that Hardy and Enever planted that dead man in the sheriff's office. The man looked like Mersey, so they got away with it. But what did they do with Mersey? They took him out to Jeff Hardy's and kept him for four days. They was makin' a bargain with him. If he'd drop the murder charge against Enever and come in with them, then he'd get his slice of loot when they took over the Basin. If he refused, they'd"—here Lugan put his finger to his temple and moved his thumb, like the falling hammer of a gun. "Nobody would miss him. He was dead anyway."

"Unh-hunh," Kelso said. "Mersey sold out for a share. They needed law."

Lugan nodded. He walked out to the edge of the cottonwoods and looked in all directions, then came back. Kelso was squatted on his haunches by the fire, his breakfast forgotten. He glanced over at Lugan and said, "Tell me more about this."

"What's there to tell?" Lugan said idly.

"They aim to take us nesters' places?"

"They aim to take all our places," Lugan said. "Yours along with ours." He laughed contemptuously. "Where's your beef now?"

"Why—on Ox-Bow range."

"Ever expect to get it back?"

Kelso sat there immobile, staring at him. He did not reply.

"You're just suckers," Lugan said calmly. "He's usin' you to whip Sands. When you've done that you'll find that you've traded masters, is all. When Sands is whipped he's goin' to pull out. Those deeds to nester places won't do him any good. Hardy and Enever will buy them up. Then they can freeze you out, because you haven't got any way to grass except over their range—or Keith's. If you kick about it there's Will Mersey, a deputy sheriff, to shut your mouth on a rustlin' charge. It's simple."

Kelso didn't say anything, only stared at him, then at his companion. Then he said shrewdly, "You don't seem worried enough about it to do much, Lugan."

"Do much?" Lugan echoed testily. "What do you think I'm on the dodge for?"

"You? On the dodge?"

"Have you seen me around here for the last three days?"

"No."

"I'm tryin' to keep from gettin' a slug in my back," Lugan said sourly. "I talked to Martha Kincaid two nights ago. They found it out. They're huntin' me now."

Kelso sat down, his legs crossed tailor-fashion under him. Again Lugan walked out to the edge of the cottonwoods and looked in all directions as if he were on guard. When he came back Kelso was sifting dirt through his fingers in absent, loose gestures, his eyes speculative. Lugan could tell he was turning all this over in his mind, letting it convince him.

"What do you aim to do?" Kelso finally asked.

"Ride out south and tell the U.S. Commissioner's office what happened to their deputy U.S. marshal," Lugan said.

"Why, dammit man! the hombre who was found dead in Mersey's office was the marshal! They killed him! He's the man that Borden sent for! He's the man Tim Enever claims he is—only, he claims he's an Association man. If he claimed he was a marshal he'd have to show his papers."

"Well, by God!" Kelso said softly.

"You couldn't spare any grub, could you?" Lugan asked.

Kelso looked around him and shrugged. "This is the last of it right here." But he was not thinking of that; his face showed it. He was studying Lugan with quiet intentness.

"Seems to me like you could settle this an easier way than callin' in the law."

"Shootin' Enever, you mean?"

"Why not?"

"A damn good reason," Lugan said grimly. "I can't get within gunshot of him. He's always suspected me, and now he knows I'm wise." He shook his head. "Not me. Somebody else could do it right enough, but not me." He didn't look at Kelso for a half a minute, then glanced obliquely at him. Kelso was still looking at him.

"He wouldn't suspect me, would he?" Kelso asked.

Lugan pretended to think a moment, then said gravely. "No, I don't see how he could."

Kelso thought about that a minute and then shook his head. "No, I ain't a gun fighter. And he is."

"Anybody could do it," Lugan said. "I've got the only thing it takes to get him off by himself—say in a dark cabin, or such, where there's another man planted."

"What's that?"

Lugan drew out Martha Kincaid's neckerchief. "Recognize that?"

Kelso nodded. "I've saw her wear it lots of times."

"He's lookin' for her, isn't he?"

"Says he is," Kelso admitted.

"If you was to slip this to him some night and tell him you ran across her and she gave it to you along with a message, what would happen?"

"What kind of message?"

"Oh, that she wants to parley with him—alone—and in Keith's shack." Lugan watched Kelso closely, his breath held.

"Yeah," Kelso said softly. "Sure." He reached out to take

the neckerchief. "Two of you could do it," Lugan said, looking at Kelso's companion. "I'd like to help, too."

Kelso stood up and spat. "What the hell are we waitin' for?" he asked mildly. "I ain't got but a quarter section of bog, but damned if I'll let any murderin' son take it from me without I got somethin' to say about it. Where is Enever?"

"Better ask at the Ox-Bow."

"We'll make it tomorrow night at Keith's?"

"That's all right with me."

Kelso looked at his companion. "Wally, you want in on this?"

"Sure."

"Then you stick here and slip out tomorrow night. Me, I'm goin' now."

Lugan watched them go to their horses. Kelso rode off toward the Ox-Bow, Wally toward the Circle P south boundary.

When they were out of sight, Lugan fell to his knees and started wolfing the cold steaks down, not bothering to chew them in his ravenous hunger.

Suddenly he laughed, and almost choked. He knelt there coughing and choking and laughing, only later remembering to take a swig of coffee to help him—the coffee that tasted like burned turnips.

15

St Cloud was standing in the lobby doorway, smoking his after-lunch cigarette and watching the slow drizzle which had started again that noon, when he saw the rider pull into the street up by the old mill.

"Rhino," he said, without turning around.

Rhino Fields was sitting in the worn rocker by the window looking through the month-old paper. His huge body was wedged into the chair, and each time he breathed the chair creaked a little. In reading, his face lost none of its utter repose, its sleepy and hard-bitten blankness. It was a tough face, craggy and strong, but overlaid with fat that seemed to paralyze its muscles. It was as if he were trying to read his paper without letting an observer suspect he was doing so. His shirt was collarless, and the suit he wore was as shapeless as a used feed sack. He looked up when St Cloud spoke.

"Where are they?" St Cloud asked.

"Asleep."

"Watch it. Someone's coming."

Rhino grunted and shifted his eyes back to his paper.

Tim Enever didn't pull up at the porch, but rode on to the big pine beside the hotel. He left his horse there out of the rain and walked over to the porch. His eyes were red rimmed and his face, under its thick stubble of black whiskers, was a little gray under its tan. His slicker was open.

St Cloud, stepping aside, knew him immediately, and he felt a cold coiling of his stomach.

"Howdy," Tim said.

St Cloud nodded. He reached for a toothpick in his vest and put it in his mouth as Tim passed him, going into the lobby. St Cloud didn't turn around when he heard Tim stop.

Rhino Fields looked up from his paper. He regarded Tim carefully, photographing him in his memory, and then went back to his paper.

"Can a man get somethin' to eat around here?" Tim asked.

Rhino put down his paper. "This ain't a hotel."

"I didn't ask that," Tim said. "I'll pay or not, just as you like. I'm hungry."

"All right," Rhino said. Without raising his voice he called: "Woman!"

In a moment the Ute woman appeared in the dining-room

door. Rhino spoke to her in Ute and she disappeared again, not even looking at Tim. Rhino was again reading his paper. Tim looked around the lobby, his eyes searching for some clue, some sign. In a dozen line camps during the past three days they had done the same thing. But there had been no sign of her, nothing to hint where she had gone. This might be different; there were rooms in this place—and there was that rider he had passed out on the porch. A Sands man? He couldn't tell. Jeff told him that Peavey was a strange place, and that Rhino Fields was a closemouthed man, and crooked.

"I'd like a bed, too," Tim said.

Rhino didn't look up from his paper this time. "This ain't a hotel," he repeated.

"You've got a second story here. Aren't there beds up there?"

"No."

Tim watched him. Rhino was looking at him, his eyes inscrutable, opaque.

Tim nodded his head toward St Cloud. "He your son?"

"No."

"Then where does he sleep?"

Rhino shook out his paper and looked at it. "Same place you will, if you stay. On the floor by the stove in the kitchen."

"I doubt that," Tim drawled.

"You likely do," Rhino said in flat voice. He called: "You, out there on the porch!"

St Cloud stepped inside the doorway.

"You can clear the hell out of here this afternoon," Rhino said to St Cloud. He regarded St Cloud with his close-set eyes for a moment, then shuttled his glance to Tim, then picked up his paper and shook it.

"What for?" St Cloud said.

"I'll hide any man that claims Jack Winters for a friend," Rhino said. "But damned if I will hide a pair of hard cases that don't trust me."

"Pair? I don't know this man," St Cloud said tonelessly, nodding toward Tim.

"You're a damned liar," Rhino said placidly. He hoisted his huge bulk to a standing position, reached in his pocket, drew out some coins and slapped them on the counter and looked again at St Cloud.

"There's your money. I said clear out and I mean it." He went into the dining room.

Tim looked at St Cloud with an expression of puzzlement. "What's the matter with him?"

"I told him I was alone," St Cloud said. "He thinks we're together."

"What if we were?"

St Cloud looked at him carefully. "He thinks we don't trust him." When Tim still looked blank, St Cloud explained. "He thinks you hid in the brush out there and sent me in ahead to see if he was on the level. Lots of these old outlaws that will hide you out are really bounty hunters. They'll shoot you in the back for the price on your head. But Rhino is on the level. He thinks we didn't trust him, though, and he's sore."

"So he throws you out?"

St Cloud nodded. "We just happened to come in too close together, I reckon."

"So you came in this mornin', too?" Tim asked.

St Cloud didn't answer immediately. He was staring at the dining-room door. "Over the mountains," he said. "Where'll you go?"

"I'm not on the dodge."

St Cloud looked at him as if he didn't believe him. "All right," St Cloud said. He walked out onto the porch again. The Ute woman came in after Tim had taken off his slicker. "Food is ready," she said.

Tim, St Cloud and Rhino all sat at the same table. St Cloud, who had just eaten, couldn't eat more. Rhino ate two big plates of food. Not once did Rhino or St Cloud look at each other.

It was the strangest situation Tim had ever walked into. He had come here suspicious. St Cloud's presence had made him more so. And then Rhino had declared himself, and it turned out that St Cloud was an outlaw on the dodge, and that he himself was suspected by Rhino of being St Cloud's partner. If he hadn't been so tired he would have laughed.

When St Cloud drank his coffee he rose. "You're makin' a mistake, Rhino," St Cloud said quietly. "I never saw him before in my life."

Rhino said quietly, "Get out of here while you can."

Without another word St Cloud left the room. Out in the lobby a few minutes later Rhino and Tim watched him ride out into the timber.

Rhino turned on Tim, "You, too," he said.

Tim grinned wearily. He was on the wrong track, and Martha wasn't here, and there was no use in arguing with Rhino. He would have liked to sleep the clock around here, but there was nothing to stop Rhino from putting a slug in his head as he slept.

"All right," Tim said.

He got his slicker under Rhino's watchful gaze. "I don't think you ever knew Jack Winters," Rhino said. "Neither of you."

"That's right," Tim said.

He went out to his horse, mounted and rode out of Peavey, cutting down toward the Ox-Bow. Rhino watched him out of sight and then went back into the dining room and from the sideboard drew out a jug of whisky. He poured himself a full tumbler and drank it off, then wiped the sweat from his brow. That was cutting things a little too fine. He wondered what would have happened if Martha Kincaid had walked into the dining room when they were eating. From the looks of Enever—for St Cloud had signaled the rider's identity—anything might have happened, and all of it unpleasant.

By dark Tim was so tired he had to sleep. He built a big fire, staked out his pony, drank his fill in the creek and came back and rolled into his blankets, and did not move until late next morning.

He made the Ox-Bow by the next evening, dead tired. There were no lights in the main house, which argued that Jeff had not finished his search of the line camps in the north Tornadoes. And that meant that Martha had not been found. He had not realized how much he had counted on Jeff finding Martha, but now that he saw that dark house his hopes sank like a stone.

Sands—if he had taken her—could have moved her under guard many miles south and out of the Basin. Certain it was that she was not here. The same thought kept recurring to him, and he could not force it out of his mind. Suppose Sands was telling the truth? Suppose she really did sell out to him, sick of all this misery and blood and fighting? Was that anything against her, that she wanted a little peace? Justice made him answer that it was not, that she was entitled to her own life, but some hot loyalty in him refused to allow him to believe that she had deserted them.

The bunkhouse was lighted up, and the mournful strains of an accordion drifted across the corral. Tim took the saddle off his tired pony, forked down some hay from the open loft and then stepped outside the corral.

"Enever," a voice said out of the dark.

Tim wheeled, his hand streaking to his gun. He stood motionless until he made out the figure of a man against the corral.

"Who is it?"

"Kelso."

Tim had a vague memory of one of the poorer nesters, a man whom he had instinctively disliked in spite of Martha's loyalty to her kind.

"What is it?"

"I seen Miss Kincaid."

Tim took two swift steps to face him. *"You what?"*

Kelso recoiled a little. "I seen Miss Kincaid. Here. She

said to give this to you." He held something out and Tim took it.

He could not see what it was and he struck a match. There in his hand was her neckerchief and its turquoise ring.

"She was wearin' that the mornin' she disappeared," Tim said aloud. He looked up into Kelso's face just as the match died. "Where did you see her?"

"In the badlands."

"How? Talk, man!"

"I was ridin' through 'em and I heard somebody call. I stopped, and Miss Kincaid, she come down off the rock rim. She asked me if I'd take a message to you and I said 'Goddlemighty, yes, he's been huntin' you for days. We all have.' She says, 'I can't come out. But will you have him meet me in Keith's cabin tonight?' I said yes. I tried——"

"What for?" Tim asked swiftly.

"I dunno. She looked mighty peekid and I asked her to come along home with me, but she wouldn't." He paused. "She's scared."

"Of what?"

"She wouldn't say. She said not to tell anybody I seen her and then she give me her neckerchief, so's to prove to you I'd seen her."

"When was it you saw her?"

"This mornin'. Early, around daylight."

"Have you got a horse here?"

"Yes."

"Get it, we'll ride over now."

Kelso disappeared. Tim went back to the corral, lighted the lantern on the nail of the loft post, and by its light, cut out and saddled a fresh horse. His hands were trembling with excitement. She was here, alive—and scared. Of what?

He questioned Kelso closely as they rode, but Kelso could tell him nothing. No, she didn't look as if she was a prisoner. Did he ask her? No, but there was nobody around. What about her food? He didn't know, but she looked like she'd been eatin' regular, just a little "peekid." Didn't she tell him any more? No, she kept lookin' around, as if she didn't want anybody to see her. Then she went back up the slope.

It was all a mystery to Tim. She was hiding from some-one, but he could not guess why. At a little past midnight they rounded the end of the badlands and headed east to Keith's place.

Once in the canyon where the house was, Tim became a little cautious. "There's no light there," he said, searching the foothills for a light.

Kelso pulled up. "You reckon it's a trap?" he asked inno-cently.

"Don't be a fool, man," Tim said sharply. "Trap for what? Martha is more loyal than any one of us. Come on."

They rode slowly up to the house. Still, it was dark and silent. Kelso laughed. "Hell, she ain't here."

They both dismounted and walked toward the shack. Tim paused at the door. "Martha!"

No sound.

Kelso whipped a match across his seat, passed Tim and stepped inside and held the match high. "Nobody here," he said.

He looked toward the other room, kicked open the door and disappeared.

Tim stepped inside. In mid-stride he heard a whisper of cloth scraping the wall to his right. He melted to the floor, just a split second before the blast of a shotgun cut loose with a bellow not five feet from his head. He lay there ut-terly motionless, as the door swung shut and plaster started to sift down to the floor in a sandy whisper.

There was a long silence, and no movement. Why didn't Kelso do something? Was it a set gun? He tried not to move as he reached down and drew out his six gun.

Suddenly Kelso's voice from the other room whispered, "Get him, Wally?"

There was no immediate answer. Tim held the gun up,

waiting for someone to strike a match. His breath was slow, quiet as he could make it.

"I dunno," a trembling voice said.

Tim shot at the sound, in the direction of the voice, and then rolled over three times. The shotgun boomed again, spreading a great mushroom of fire out into the room. Tim snapped three shots at it and then stood up. Kelso's shots from the other room kicked up dirt into Tim's boot.

There was sudden silence. Then someone over by the door said, "Ah-h-h-h," in a long, tired, gurgling sigh and there was a rough scraping of cloth on plaster, the sound of a body collapsing.

Tim watched the partition door now. Suddenly two orange flashes boomed in it, and Tim felt the slugs pound into the plaster beside him. He heard Kelso scamper for cover, and then he tiptoed quietly toward the downed figure.

"I'm comin' in and get you, Kelso," Tim said in a thick, quiet way, his voice sounding large in that silence. There was no answer.

Tim's foot touched a body. He paused, holding his gun toward it, but it did not move. He stopped and groped blindly for the shotgun and found it, his eyes on the darkness that was the partition of the doorway.

Now he was fumbling for shells in the downed man's pocket. He found two, and softly loaded the shotgun.

Then he stood up and moved out to the center of the room.

"I'm comin', Kelso," he said swiftly. He took two steps to the right. "I've got the shotgun now."

There was utter silence again. He thought he could hear Kelso breathing loudly in the next room, but he could not be certain it was not his own breathing. He waited until his heart had stopped slugging against his ribs, and then he lay down on his belly. Slowly, with infinite care, he wormed toward the door, wary of every move.

"Enever," Kelso said in a husky whisper from inside the other room. "I give up."

Tim said nothing. He felt the door sill under his hand and pulled himself forward until he figured his shoulders were through the doorway. Kelso was not going to give up, not going to surrender to him, not while he had a shell in a gun or the strength to pull a trigger. A cold rage held him taut as wire, and his senses were keen, predatory.

Kelso didn't speak again. He knew he was a doomed man. There was not a sound, not even the sound of breathing, for Kelso was probably breathing through his mouth, as Tim was.

Tim lay there for two full minutes, working his six gun out of its holster. He grabbed it by the barrel, then raised his left hand far over his head, and using the gun as a club, tapped twice on the doorjamb. There was no sound, nothing in that tar black to indicate a man was there.

Tim wanted another half minute, his nerves edging him. Then he crawled on through the door and straight on into the room, moving with infinite caution, expecting at any moment to reach out and touch Kelso's boots. When he was five feet inside the room, he rose, and taking his six-gun, waited.

He tried to listen, to hear, until the very silence roared in his ears. He could hear nothing. Was Kelso gone?

He took his gun in his left hand, faced the door and cast it from him. It clanked on the sill.

Immediately, close on the floor, a gun belched fire. In its half-second flash, Tim saw Kelso lying full length against the wall away from the door, shooting blindly up into the doorway.

He brought his shotgun hip high and emptied both barrels at Kelso. He was so sure of his shots that he did not even dodge.

When the roar died in his ears he heard the slow tap of a boot on the dirt, and he felt a little sick. He must have passed within three feet of Kelso, both of them on their bellies, when he crawled through the door.

He made no pretense of silence now. He fumbled for a

match, struck it, picked up his six gun, not looking at Kelso, and went into the other room. He saw the man lying against the wall by the window, and he walked over to him and knelt by him.

He rolled him over and studied the face. Where had he seen it before?

And then, like a crash of lightning, a gun blasted in the window. Tim felt something slam into his shoulder and rake down his back, the violence of it setting him over backward. His match dropped. In that falling, he shot once through the window in the dark, heard a grunt, then the pounding of feet as somebody ran. He got to his feet, staggered and fell, and tried to get up again. Even the darkness was pin-wheeling before his eyes. He yanked the door open and sprawled out into the dirt. Out there in the darkness, out by the corral, he heard a man running. His step was broken, and Tim could hear him grunt softly, as if with pain. He had been hit, Tim guessed.

Tim got to his feet and tried to run and went down again, and when he was lying there on the ground he heard the man ride off. Tim fought to his feet and made it to the corral. There, weaving on his feet, he struck a match and studied the ground. There was a trail of dark spots in the dirt which Tim knew to be blood.

A kind of stubborn fury had hold of Tim. If the man was hit he might go down off there in the night. And Tim was going to see who he was. He went to his horse, mounted, and set out after him.

Tim's slug caught Lugan just below his left ribs. After the shot at Tim, Lugan had straightened up, wheeling away from the low window, and then Tim's slug slammed into him, staggering him. By the time he achieved his horse real panic had seized him. He had to get out of here.

Once he was away from Keith's place, he stopped to take stock of his wound. While he was feeling it gingerly he heard a horseman coming. His head yanked up and he listened. Yes, that damn Enever was on his trail. He roweled his pony and set off in a pounding gallop. The next hour for John Lugan was the worst he ever spent in his life. He was never wholly out of earshot of Tim's horse. All the tricks he had ever learned in covering his trail were used to no avail. Tim hung onto him like a leech, almost sensing his very thoughts. Sick, afraid, Lugan thought some strange things that night. He began to wonder if Tim Enever was human, if he could be killed. When he realized he was thinking these half-delirious thoughts he knew he would have to pull himself together, shake Enever and get home.

He made a circle back into the edge of the badlands, entered, made a wide circle in them, came out where he went in and rode hard for home. When he touched the creek, he rode in it for three miles, coming out of it below his place and circling back. Yet he had a feeling that almost amounted to panic that he had not succeeded in shaking Tim, and that he would ride in here presently.

So he made his plans accordingly. He turned his pony loose outside the corral, slapped him in the rump and watched him trot off into the darkness of the pasture. His saddle he chucked into the loft and covered with hay.

On his way to the house he stopped at the cookshack and got a cup of flour. Once in his room he leaned against the wall, breathing deeply, waiting for strength to return. Only cold terror kept him on his feet, fighting against the blackness he knew was going to down him sooner or later.

He undressed in his room, shedding his bloody clothes. His next act was to yank a blanket off his bed and try to tear it. He was too weak. In desperation, he hunted for something to cut it with, and then thought of his hunting knife in the drawer under his clean clothes. He got it out, cut a wide strip off the blanket and put the knife on the table again. Then he took the flour and pressed it against his wound. It was bleeding slowly, aching like fire, but the flour clotted the blood and stopped the flow of it. Then he wound the strip of blanket tightly around him, covering the wound.

He was getting weaker but he fought on. He got some water and washed the blood from his legs and feet, then he climbed into a fresh suit of underwear. Over it he pulled an unsoiled pair of jeans. He contrived to put the basin of water under the bed, kick his bloody clothes alongside it, then he fell into bed and blew out the light. But he could not sleep. Tim was coming—and this little play had to be acted out. He could not faint now. He took a stiff drink of whisky from the bottle by his bed and lay there waiting.

And Tim did come. He came before the lamp chimney was cold. He hammered on the door of Lugan's cabin with the butt of his gun.

Lugan gathered all his remaining strength and got up. He lighted the lamp and looked around him for any sign of blood. There was none. A glance in the mirror told him that the blanket around his middle was holding the flour in place, and that the blanket was invisible under his underwear. He saw the knife on the table, swept it to the floor and kicked it under the table.

He took a deep breath, picked up the lamp in one hand, his gun in the other, tramped out into the living room and threw the door open.

Tim Enever was standing there, his eyes like hot coals in a face that was gray with pain. He had a gun in one hand, and his other hand was covered with blood.

They looked at each other for a long second, and Lugan kept his eyes steady, although his knees were trembling.

He asked at last, in a curious, almost hushed voice, "What the hell has happened to you, Enever?"

"You don't know?" Tim said softly, meaningly.

"You're all over blood."

"That's right," Tim said slowly, watching Lugan's face. But it was inscrutable.

"Want me to call the boys?" Lugan asked.

"No, don't bother," Tim murmured. He was standing in the circle of light cast by Lugan's lamp. He was waiting— waiting for one single sign that would give Lugan away. He had lost the trail three miles back at the creek, lost it completely, but by that time his suspicion had crystallized. A search for tracks confirmed it. The rider had entered this creek and come out where? Lugan's place was the closest, the most obvious.

But there was nothing in Lugan's face to indicate it, except a pinched expression around the nostrils. Moreover, there was no blood on him—and the gulcher was hit. Suspicion died hard in Tim, and reluctantly, for it was fanned by anger that was not even dimmed.

"Where you been tonight, Lugan?" he asked softly.

"In bed."

"Before that."

"What the hell's that to you?" Lugan asked testily.

Tim raised his gun a little. "Plenty. Where were you?"

"In town," Lugan said surlily.

"You look a little sick, Lugan," Tim murmured.

"I ought to. I got drunk at the Gem." He paused. "What's the matter with you?"

"Three jaspers tried to beef me tonight," Tim said quietly. "I killed two. I'm lookin' for the third."

Lugan hesitated just long enough, then said sourly, "And you think I'm the third?"

"I don't know what to think," Tim answered him, watching him, watching him for any sign, any clue.

But Lugan was acting with a finesse born of desperation. He said testily, "Then get the hell out of here! You've had your look!"

"Not yet," Tim murmured, lifting his gun. "Not yet. I want a good look."

"At what?"

"Your house."

Lugan glared at him and cursed him. "I ought to pistol whip you, Enever. If you weren't so sick I would." He threw the door open and stood aside. "Look wherever you like, only make it quick—good and damn quick!"

Tim walked into the bedroom. Yes, the bed was slept on.

There was the whisky by the side of Lugan's bed. Boots, socks, shirt and hat were scattered over the room, like a drunk man would throw them. He felt his anger die, and a great feeling of weariness came over him. He had missed after coming so close.

He turned and walked back to the door by which Lugan was still standing, holding the lamp. "All right," Tim said. "I'm wrong."

"Hell with you," Lugan said curtly. "Get out!"

Tim walked out and climbed on his horse. Lugan stood in the doorway in his bare feet just long enough to see Tim ride out into the night, and he closed the door. He saw the room wheeling in front of him. Some instinctive caution prompted him to blow out the lamp. It was just in time.

The floor seemed to rise up and hit him in the face, and he heard a faint tinkle of glass before blessed blackness enveloped him.

16

His men found him that way the next morning, sprawled on the floor behind the closed door, the shattered lamp by his head. They lifted him into the bed, where Lugan came to.

"Drunk, I guess," he said, and smiled up at them, and they went out. Lugan lay there half awake, taking stock of the situation. Today, his week's grace from Sands was up. He tried to think of what to do, and went to sleep. When he awakened the cook was standing over him.

"Gent to see you, boss."

"Who?"

"Some hard case. Never seen him before."

"Tell him to come in."

Lugan swung his feet out of bed and reached for his gun and hid it under the covers. He was pulling on his boots and socks when the man entered. It was one of Sands' riders.

"Boss wants to see you," the rider said.

"Oh, he does, does he?" Lugan drawled. "I don't want to see him. Tell him so for me, will you?"

The rider's face didn't change. "You comin' with me?"

"No," Lugan said flatly. "I am not. I don't——" His speech stopped. He had just thought of something. He looked closely at the man. "Have those new men come back with Sands?" he asked.

The rider looked as if he wasn't sure if he should answer. Finally he said, "Some. The rest are comin' in tomorrow."

Lugan nodded. "All right. Beat it."

"You ain't comin'?"

"Tell Sands to go to hell. Now get out of here."

The rider went out and Lugan heaved himself to his feet. His side had a dull ache in it and it was stiff, but beyond that he felt all right. He took a drink of whisky and sat down on the bed again.

This, he guessed, was the pay-off. He hadn't killed Enever and he had told Sands, his boss, to go to hell. It would only be a matter of hours before Sands got word to the ranchers that it was Lugan who had betrayed them. He scratched his thatch of curly hair and yawned. He was at the end of his rope, but strangely enough, he didn't feel bad about it. Nevertheless, he would have to get out of here. If he wasn't out of this Basin in another three hours he was a dead man.

That being so, he sat there and thought what he ought to do about it. Where could he go? Wasn't there some way he could even things up with Sands before he left? Yes, he could warn the ranchers that Sands had thousands of sheep coming down the Tornadoes and thirty hired gunmen on the way to join him in a savage series of raids. That was something. It would hurt Sands a little, maybe defeat him, but that wasn't what Lugan was thinking of. He wanted to hurt him for good, permanently; he wanted to ruin him. He wanted to——

Ah, Julie Sands!

If he got Julie and took her away it would kill Sands! He would turn over heaven and earth to get her back; he would pay anything. Lugan laughed aloud at the thought. Money, that's what he wanted. And Julie Sands would be worth more than a gold mine to him. She was up at Peavey, lightly guarded, his for the taking.

He stood up and began to pace the room, his eyes bright with excitement. Then he got a sheet of paper, a pencil and sat down to write a note.

ENEVER: (it began) *I been in Sands' pay from the first. We planned to wipe out your ranchers and take this valley over between us. My job was to kill you, and last night I failed. Sands can't use me any more, so he's going to betray me to you. I wanted to get in ahead of him. And I want to hurt him as much as I can.*

He's bringin' thousands more sheep down the Tornadoes and they're on the way now and he's got thirty gunmen coming.

Now Enever heres a tip for what its worth. Sands is going to get word to you that Im a trator. Dont you let him get to you to tell you. That will make him mad and he'll think Im safe over here with you. What will he do? He'll raid my place and try to get me. There's where you come in.

Fort up all your men around my place and lay in wait for him. When them gunnies of his ride up to my place to kill me you have got them. I don't know but what Sands may come with them so theres yore chance to get him.

None of my men was in on this so dont hurt them. I'm getting out of the country pronto. All this is the truth as you can see and beleeve me my tip is good. Trap him at my place. You cant lose by trying it.

JOHN LUGAN

Lugan folded the note, hunted for an envelope and found it and then set about dressing. At the last he looked around for anything valuable to take with him and found that in a lifetime of living in this Basin there was nothing he wanted to take out of it—except money.

He went out, called one of his hands, told him to ride over to the corral and cut out his best horse and saddle it. His side hurt him a little when he rode, and he wondered if he should risk a trip into town to see Doc Masters. He voted against it; Doc would only start it bleeding again. Right now, it was clotted, and it must be a clean wound because it didn't feel like it was infected.

He rode off his range, not even bothering to take a last look at the place, and headed up the mountains for Peavey. He rode steadily all through the day and into the night, stopping only occasionally to rest his side.

He rode into Peavey a couple of hours before daylight. The hotel was utterly dark, but he rode boldly up to the porch, dismounted, and hammered on the door with the butt of his gun. In a few minutes he saw the faint light cast by the lamp through the window. It grew stronger. Then the door inched open and Rhino's face showed through it. He was holding the lamp over his head, examining Lugan.

Lugan shoved at the door and said, "Where's St Cloud?"

"Who wants him?"

"Sands, you damn fool! Open up!"

Rhino swung the door wide and Lugan entered the lobby. "Where's he sleepin'?"

From the stairs came St Cloud's voice. "What's the matter?"

Lugan wheeled and looked up at him. St Cloud had on a pair of pants, and he held a gun in his hand.

"I want to talk to you alone," Lugan said.

"Beat it, Rhino," St Cloud said. Rhino put his lamp on the desk and went out through the dining room.

Lugan said, "Enever and Hardy with five men are on their way up here now. I had an hour's start on them."

"Here? What for?"

"Miss Kincaid, you jug head!" Lugan said. He looked at St Cloud. "Well, you goin' to move 'em?"

"I reckon we got to," St Cloud said. "Come on up and tell me about it."

He led the way upstairs and back through the dark corridor to his room. A candle burned on the table beside his cot. He sat down and started pulling on his boots as Lugan began. "Well, I was over at the Ox-Bow when Enever rode in." He moved a couple of steps toward St Cloud.

"Yeah, he was up here," St Cloud said. His head was bent over. One boot under the bed had escaped him.

Lugan drew out his gun and said, "Well, he and Hardy got to talking——" He moved two steps closer to St Cloud. St Cloud swore and went down on all fours.

"Yeah?"

Lugan brought his gun barrel down across St Cloud's head. St Cloud melted to the floor and didn't even move. Lugan looked at him a moment to make sure it was a good job, then he rose and went out into the hall. He paused to make sure there was a key in the door.

"Miss Kincaid!" he called, his voice booming down the corridor. He paced it slowly, listening, calling again. Presently, ahead of him, a door opened.

Martha, a blanket wrapped around her, stood in the doorway, her lamp in her hand. When she saw him, her jaws clicked together with a slight noise.

"Come with me," Lugan said curtly. "St Cloud's sick."

Martha hesitated, but he had swung around and was going down the hall. Martha followed. Lugan stood aside, allowing her to go into the room. She did, and he closed the door behind her.

"I'm gettin' out of here with Julie Sands," Lugan said levelly. His tone of voice jerked Martha's attention from St Cloud. She looked at him, and his face was ugly with excitement.

"I'd hate to have to hit you, Miss Kincaid," he said

quickly. "If you make any noise I will, though. I'm going to tie you up and gag you. I want a good head start."

Martha backed away.

"What'll it be," Lugan asked calmly. His forehead was beaded with sweat, and his eyes were hard, calculating.

Martha wondered if she should take a chance, and then she wondered who there was to help her. Not Rhino. If he came up he'd get shot, and not Julie. She was as helpless as Martha herself.

"All right," Martha said. "I'll do it on one condition— that you answer one question for me—and answer it truthfully, if you know how."

"Go ahead. Ask."

"Is Tim Enever all right?"

Lugan smiled uglily. "Yes, damn him! I tried to kill him last night and almost got killed instead. Does that answer your question?"

"He's all right?"

"He's hurt a little. Not much."

"Thank God," Martha said. "All right, I'm ready."

Lugan whipped a blanket from St Cloud's cot and ripped it. After tearing off several strips, he told Martha to stand still. He trussed her firmly, hands and feet, then laid her on the cot. St Cloud's bandanna was used for her gag. Lugan was in a hurry; his fingers trembled as he tried to gauge the tightness of the gag.

Finished, he did not say another word but wheeled out of the door, slamming it behind him. It did not catch, and slowly swung open again, so that Martha could hear him stamp down the hall, calling, "Miss Julie! Miss Julie!"

Martha heard Julie's door open. "What is it?" Julie asked sleepily.

"You've got to get dressed," Lugan said. "We're traveling."

"Who are you?"

"One of your dad's men. The ranchers have discovered

this hide-out and they're on their way here now. You've got to hurry."

"Where's St Cloud?"

"He's gone ahead with Miss Kincaid. Now hurry. I'll go get the horses."

"All right," Julie said wearily. "Where are we going?"

"Over the mountains. Those are my instructions. Now hurry, please."

Lugan tramped down the stairs. Martha heard several things then. One of them was Lugan out at the barn ripping off the lock on the shed and bringing out the horse and saddling it. Another was Julie. Her footsteps came down as far as Martha's room, and Martha could almost see her looking in.

Martha tried desperately to move enough to make some sound that would attract Julie, but she could not move, could not make a noise. Julie went back to her room, spent a little while there, and then Martha heard her go downstairs.

The lobby door opened then and Lugan said, "You go outside. I've got something to settle with Rhino."

"Are you sure Miss Kincaid and St Cloud have gone?"

"Certain. I woke them first. Miss Kincaid is the one the ranchers are after, so she went first."

"Considerate," Julie said dryly.

Martha heard her go out. There was a brief silence, then Lugan called, "Rhino!" Martha could even hear Rhino's ponderous step through the kitchen into the dining room. Suddenly there was a shot, and then another. Its echo hammered through the corridors, and then Martha heard the lobby door close. There was a brief silence, then the pounding of horses' hooves as Julie and Lugan left.

Then the sounds diminished momentarily. There was movement downstairs, and then Martha heard a woman sobbing. That was Rhino's wife.

Suddenly she heard Rhino say in a tight voice, "Don't squat here and bawl, damn it! Help me up and stop this bleedin'."

There were long series of sounds after that, none of them indicating that the Ute woman or Rhino remembered St Cloud or herself. Martha set to work then to struggle out of her bonds.

It took her till daylight, and when she was finished her wrists were bloody. Her first move was to take out the gag and work saliva into her mouth, then she set about freeing herself. The next thing she did was to steal into her room and dress. She kept telling herself all this while that this was her chance to leave, to escape. But all the time she knew that she couldn't leave St Cloud in there. He was alive, because she had felt his heart beat. But he was hurt.

When she was finished dressing she had made up her mind. She tiptoed back through the silent corridor and closed the door to St Cloud's room behind her.

First she got his gun, made sure it was loaded, then laid it on the table. There was a pitcher of water on the table. She took this and poured half its contents in St Cloud's face, then picked up the gun and stepped back.

St Cloud's eyes opened and for a full half minute he stared at the ceiling. A movement of hers attracted his gaze and he stared at her for a moment, then pulled himself to a sitting position. Martha had the gun in her hand.

"What's that for?" St Cloud asked.

"I'm going."

St Cloud scowled. "What happened? Lugan—Lugan." He couldn't remember.

"He slugged you over the head, then tied me up and gagged me. He shot Rhino, too. He's taken Julie."

"Julie!" St Cloud struggled to his feet, oblivious to the gun in Martha's hand. "Where did he take her?"

"I don't know." Martha told him what she had overheard Lugan tell Julie, and as she talked the color came back in St Cloud's face and there was murder in his eyes.

When she was finished, St Cloud said quietly, "Thanks, Miss Kincaid."

He looked at the gun. "You won't need that, and I will. Can't I have it?"

"What are you going to do?"

"Murder Lugan when I get him." His eyes clouded. "If he's hurt her——" He didn't finish.

"St Cloud," Martha said suddenly, "are you in love with Julie?"

St Cloud looked her full in the eye and nodded. "Yes. I always have been, only she wouldn't wipe her feet on my kind. I don't care now. I'm goin' to get Lugan and turn her loose—loose from her father, I mean. I'll take her anywhere she wants to go to get away from him." He smiled thinly. "After that, I'm comin' back to Tornado Basin and fight—fight on your side, I mean."

"Against Sands?"

"That's what I mean," St Cloud said. "I'm a cowman. I may be tough and not much good, but I'm too good to fight for a sheepman." He looked at the gun again. "I got to hurry, Miss Kincaid. Can I have my gun?"

"What are you going to do about me?"

"Nothing—only saddle your horse so you can ride back to your friends."

Martha knew it might have been a trick to disarm her; she also knew, deep within her, that she had seen a turning point in a man's life. She handed him the gun. He smiled, slipped it into his holster and said, "We haven't much time. I haven't, I mean."

"Is your head all right?"

St Cloud nodded. "For the first time in my life," he said wryly, and smiled. Martha laughed with him.

Downstairs, Rhino was lying on blankets on the floor of the dining room. St Cloud went up to him and said, "Rhino, we're pullin' out."

Rhino's eyes looked sick. His wife was sitting by him, and she said nothing.

"You backed the wrong man, Rhino," St Cloud said. "So did I. I'm changin'."

Rhino said weakly, "You double-crosser."

St Cloud turned and went out, Martha following him. At the stable St Cloud saddled two horses, handed Martha the reins of one and said, "Good luck, Miss Kincaid."

"I hope you find her, St Cloud," Martha said. "And if you do, don't be shy."

"Shy?" St Cloud looked at her with a quizzical expression.

"Tell her you love her," Martha said calmly. "She's been waiting to hear that word all her life. Will you?"

"Why not?" St Cloud said. "It's nothin' but the truth."

17

St Cloud had stated the truth; he was a cattleman. He was not a saloon bum, either, not a gunman, bred in the smoky darkness of a gambling table. Most of his life had been spent outdoors, punching cattle, and he could read sign like an Indian. It stood him in good stead now.

He picked up Lugan's and Julie's trail immediately, and he read it expertly. He was the kind of tracker that is sometimes found in Mexico among the vaqueros; his method was part knowledge, a whole lot observation, and the rest intuition. He could read country like the printed page, and he understood instinctively where the best traveling was, where the sign was to be found. If he knew the general direction his quarry was traveling, he could leave the sign for a half day and pick it up at will, and, what was more important, he could sense a short cut.

An hour of riding Lugan's trail and he understood it. Lugan was working for the peaks. Furthermore, he was fumbling, feeling about for a pass that he had probably heard of but could not locate. When St Cloud knew that he picked the tallest tree he could find, he climbed it and spent fifteen minutes studying the heights ahead of him. All the water courses, all the cattle trails pointed straight ahead up the slope, but St Cloud could see that they were false. The real pass lay off to the south, where the gradient was gentler and where a large boulder field hid it to the naked eye.

He made his decision. Lugan would strike straight ahead, find out his path was blocked, and would cast about for the real pass. Cattle sign would tell him if he was not so stupid he could not read it. Eventually, he would come to the real pass, after a long and fumbling delay.

St Cloud headed straight for the pass. He traveled swiftly, avoiding the brush-tangled canyons, using every open-mountain meadow, saving his horse and still pushing him to a mile-eating pace.

In midafternoon, St Cloud left timber line behind him and worked his way up through the boulder field. Presently he came to the pass, a twisted canyon between high peaks. Old tracks, deer and cattle both, proved it beyond a doubt. There were no horse tracks there. St Cloud rode a half mile to the south, staked out his horse in a nest of boulders that protected him from the chill upland wind, then went back to the pass and squatted behind a boulder.

He had a long wait, so long that he thought he made a wrong guess. But when the sun started to heel over, bringing into bold relief all this upland waste of rock, he caught sight of two black specks working among the boulders. He tested the wind to make sure his scent would not alarm their horses, found it favorable, and then hunkered down to wait.

Presently he heard the sharp ring of the horses' shoes on the rock. They were tired, he could tell. It was many minutes before that sound drew close. Still, St Cloud did not move.

And then, in single file past him, they rode into the pass, Julie ahead. St Cloud let them go past him perhaps ten feet, then he stood up and said, "Lugan!"

At the sound of the voice, Julie's horse shied. Lugan pulled up, and for one brief second he did not move. St Cloud knew he was debating whether to go for his gun. But curiosity would conquer. Lugan would have to know how many men were behind him.

Lugan turned and saw St Cloud standing there, his hand with the gun hanging down at his side.

"Cut loose your dogs, Lugan, because this is payday," St Cloud said mildly.

Julie had stopped now, and was facing them.

At the same instant Lugan's hand flashed up across his body, and the sun glinted on his gun.

St Cloud shot from the hip, and he shot first. His first slug whipped into Lugan and jarred him, so that his gun went off at the ground. The first, second and third shots shook him in his saddle, and his mouth opened in a kind of panicked surprise. The last shot drove him out of the saddle onto the boulders, and he lay there on his side without moving.

St Cloud holstered his gun and walked past Lugan to where Julie's horse was standing. St Cloud took the bridle and led the horse out of sight of Lugan, then he stopped and looked up at Julie.

"I'm sorry I had to do it that way," he said.

Julie dismounted, steadying herself against St Cloud. It was a minute before she spoke, and then she said in a trembling voice, "I—he was taking me, St Cloud."

"I know."

"He was going to hold me until Dad paid him a lot of money."

St Cloud said nothing. Suddenly Julie's nerves broke. She started to sob and St Cloud folded her into his arms. He stood there stiffly, saying nothing until Julie's sobs ceased. She buried her face in his shoulder, clinging to him.

"I'm takin' you away, Julie," St Cloud said then. "Away from this bloody mess, away from that wolf of a father of yours. I'll take you anywhere you want to go."

Julie held him closely. "All right."

"I don't reckon there's much more to say," St Cloud said, looking down at the top of her head, then looking away. He wanted to caress her and kiss her, but something stopped him.

"Yes, there is," he amended quietly. "It's just this. I don't reckon I ever want to leave you, Julie. I'll stick by you and fight for you as long as you'll let me."

Julie was strangely quiet. She raised her head slowly to look into his tense face. "Do you mean that, St Cloud?" she asked. "Do you mean you'd stay with me and—and not send me to places I hate, like I was a piece of baggage."

"I'll stay with you, I said," St Cloud said stubbornly.

"But—but why?" Julie murmured. "It isn't like you, like any man, St Cloud. Why do you say that?"

St Cloud got it out. It was toneless, emotionless. "Because I ain't worth a damn when you're not around, Julie. I don't reckon I ever would be. I got you in my blood, and when I can't be with you I don't want to be anywhere else. I don't even want to be alive." He looked down at her. "I—I just love you, I reckon."

Julie looked at him for one humble moment, then she raised on tiptoe and kissed him. For one brief instant the world stopped going around for St Cloud, and then he knew what had happened. He knew without her having to say it, but she did.

"And I've loved you—always, I guess," Julie murmured. "But I never thought I could tell you. I never thought you were interested in anything but fighting and lying and bullying. I didn't know!"

"You do now," St Cloud said.

Julie looked up at him, her face changing. "Dad!" she said. "What will he do?"

St Cloud smiled grimly. "First, he's going to take a whippin', Julie. I'm goin' to help give it to him. I'm goin' down and help those poor damned cowmen, and when we've licked your dad he's goin' to be humble. He's goin' to eat crow, Julie, and my crow at that. There's just one other thing I want to do before I die—besides love you—and that's to tell that damn proud man that I'm going to take his daughter, and he's not goin' to stop me."

"Then let's hurry," Julie said calmly.

"It means I'm fighting him if we go down."

"It means we're fighting him," Julie said, a little sadly. "Let's go down."

Julie rode over to where St Cloud had staked his horse, and St Cloud went back to the pass. He piled stones on Lugan's body, and not once did he let himself think of what would have happened to Julie if he'd missed them here.

It was just getting dusk when he was finished. He started off toward his horse, and then a sudden shift of wind brought a sound to his ears. He stopped to listen, and suddenly his jaw muscles corded.

He went on, got Julie and they started out of the boulder field. Suddenly Julie pulled up her horse and said, "Listen."

"I heard it," St Cloud said.

"It's——"

"Sheep," St Cloud said. "Comin' through the pass. They're goin' back through in short order, too."

They passed through Peavey after dark on their way to the Ox-Bow. St Cloud stopped at the hotel and walked into the silent lobby. There was a lamp lighted in the dining room.

From the door St Cloud could see Rhino's great bulk stretched out on the floor. The Ute woman was sitting there beside him, and she turned great grief-stricken eyes on St Cloud.

He came over and stood above Rhino. He couldn't tell if Rhino recognized him or not, for there was nothing on Rhino's face except pain.

"I got him, Rhino," St Cloud said gently. "I thought you'd like to know."

"You rat," Rhino whispered.

St Cloud nodded thoughtfully. "That's right, a double-crossin' rat, Rhino. I've took my last fighting money from

Sands. Julie and I are gettin' married. But first we're going down to the Ox-Bow, and I'm goin' to fight Sands along with Jeff Hardy and Tim Enever."

"You damn coyote," Rhino said, his whisper implacable.

St Cloud only smiled gravely. "It's a fine feelin', Rhino—one you've never known. You can look down a road and see it's straight, not crooked. You can even see the end of it, Rhino." He shook his head. "So long, Rhino. You're an honest crook."

He went out. Rhino's eyes followed him to the door, and then they shifted to his wife.

"Get your horse," he whispered. "Ride down and tell Sands that his girl is at the Ox-Bow and that St Cloud has sold out."

"No," she said.

"You go," Rhino said sternly. He looked at her, and the old fire mounted into his eyes so that she winced under his gaze. She stood up.

"Will you be all right?" she said, falling back into Ute.

"I'm not sick," Rhino said. "I feel fine. Go on."

He knew and she knew that he was dying. She looked at him a long moment, and Rhino smiled wearily.

"Go on," he said.

She went.

18

They woke Tim up to give him Lugan's note. He was sleeping in the main house, and when he came out into the big room his hair was tousled, and he was not shaved. His shoulder where the slug took him was thick with bandage, but he looked rested—and discouraged. He read the note and then read it again, and then handed it to Jeff, who was sitting in his deep chair. "Then Sands has got Martha," Tim said, when Jeff was finished reading.

Jeff nodded. Tim stood there in the middle of the room, gazing speculatively out the window. That made a difference, he reflected, a difference that meant death to Sands.

Jeff's voice called him back. "Well?"

"I didn't hear."

"What do you think of Lugan's tip?"

"Yes," Tim said absently. He hadn't really thought; the only thing the note meant to him was that it was proof enough that Lugan had turned Martha over to Sands.

Jeff rose and came over to him and took him by the arm. "You're thinkin' the same thing I am, son. It's that we got to get her back. But have you stopped to think that Lugan might have given us the way to do it?"

Tim's glance settled on Jeff. "I hadn't. No."

"If I know Sands he'll aim to settle Lugan the first thing. And as Lugan says, he's bound to burn his place out, just for safety. All right, Sands may be with his men, like Lugan said. If we get him we as good as got Martha back, ain't we?"

Tim thought a moment. "I reckon. Sure."

Jeff looked down at the note. "If we was only sure."

A change came over Tim. He took the note and read it again and then said, "He meant it, I reckon. He hates Sands, and he's so scared of him he ran away. Any man who's that scared has got to hate the man who's responsible, Jeff."

"Then you think we ought to prepare for the raid?"

"I do."

"Then get your boots on, boy. We got some ridin' to do."

Tim made himself have patience. Every moment that he took away from hunting Martha somehow seemed a criminal waste, but he kept telling himself that this was the only weapon they had. Maybe, if they were lucky, Sands would come with his riders and would be captured.

The difficulty now was getting the other ranchers to believe that Lugan was not lying, that it was not just a trap to draw them all away from their places so Sands could raid and destroy them the more easily. Tim had a few talking points, but his main one was that since it obviously was Lugan's nature to betray men, he was running true to form in betraying Sands. It took a lot of talking and a lot of riding.

The first thing to do was to send a man down to see if Sands was gathering more riders. In the last two days the sheepmen had made a camp on the other side of the river, so that spying was possible. And Tim's scouts returned with the news that men were drifting in to swell the numbers of Sands' gunmen.

Almost reluctantly, then, the ranchers agreed to set the trap at Lugan's Fish-hook. Although none of them said it to Tim their main reason for agreeing was not because they believed they might trap Sands and his riders; it was because Tim's blind hunch had worked out in the badlands fight. Maybe it would again.

The plan was simple. Two or three scouts were to watch the bridge and report when the body of Sands' riders crossed. The others were to drift over to the Fish-hook under the cover of first darkness. There, they would turn their horses over to a wrangler who would take them a mile west of the place and corral them.

The Fish-hook, in spite of its lack of cover, was ideal for the ambush. One party of men could fort up in the barns and the corrals to the southwest. Another could take the bunkhouse to the south. The ridge to the north could hide a dozen riders and give them a wicked advantage. And the low brush along the creek to the east could hide any army.

But, what was most important of all, the house itself would be defended. It must have a light in it, and the bunkhouse must have a light, as if nothing were amiss. Eight men could hide in the house. Sands' first act—if he came— would be to come to the house and see if Lugan was there. One of Lugan's punchers would open the door. At a signal

from him the men in the house could take Sands, take him
alive, too, for a trial that would prove forever to sheepmen
that Tornado Basin was not for them. Tim, Jeff, Pete Turner, Will Mersey and the top hands from four of the outfits
were to be in the house. Proctor, Bennett, Joe Manship and
Sam Rutherford were to take care of the outside.

The one other point mentioned in Lugan's note was of
first importance. Tim must not let Sands communicate with
him in any way, so as to make it impossible to be informed
of Lugan's guilt. When Sands saw that he could not tell the
ranchers, then he would punish Lugan himself.

And twice during that day Sands' riders at the Circle P
line, waving a piece of white cloth on the end of their carbines, tried to parley with the ranchers. And twice they were
driven back by rifle fire.

The third time Sands himself tried to parley. He was
driven back, too. Every pair of boundary riders was in-
structed to shoot at the Sands' riders on sight, and to have
no communication with them.

Tim and Jeff were at Proctor's place at dusk. One by one
the boundary riders drifted in, reported, and rode out again
in the direction of the Fish-hook.

Tim and Jeff were the last to leave, for they wanted to ride
up on the place and see if it looked natural. When they came
in sight of the Fish-hook, there was a light in the
bunkhouse. Someone was strumming on a guitar there. Behind the curtains in the main house a lamp was lighted.
Down by the creek there was only a dark line to mark the
brush. All was quiet in the barns and corrals.

Jeff said, "Looks natural enough to me" and Tim agreed
with him. The horse wrangler was waiting for them at the
corner of the house, and he took their horses.

Inside the house Mersey and Pete Turner and others were
playing a nervous game of poker in the living room. Jeff
joined them, and Tim made the rounds to see if everyone
was ready. They were—except the men in the barn were

complaining because Joe Manship wouldn't let them smoke. Tim backed Joe up in his decision.

Then came the wait. It was long and nerve straining. Because Tim did not want to run the risk of having Sands' riders slip by the scouts at the bridge and come up without warning, he insisted that the men keep their places.

The poker game went on and on, each man playing with only half his attention. It was around ten o'clock when a rider pounded into the place. Tim stepped out to meet him.

"They're comin' this way," the rider said. "About twenty-five, I reckon."

"How close are they?"

"Coupla miles, maybe."

"Take your horse over and join the boys on the ridge," Tim said. He made the rounds for the last time, and then returned to the house. The poker table was cleared off and the men were in the bedroom.

It seemed like they had waited half the night before they heard the swelling murmur of many riders out on the hard-packed yard. Tim pulled the shade aside a little to look outside. A dozen or so of the riders had stopped to talk to the crew in the bunkhouse. The others were riding toward the house. Tim stepped into the partition doorway and nodded to Lugan's puncher, who was nervously awaiting the knock on the door.

It came, and it was rough, peremptory. The puncher walked over to the door and opened it and looked out.

"Lugan here?" a voice asked.

The puncher said no. He put his right hand up on the doorjamb and leaned on it, the signal that Sands was not among the riders. "Anything I can do for you?" he asked.

"Yeah. Clear out of here if you want to save your hide."

At that very moment a shot cracked out down by the bunkhouse. Afterward, Tim learned that a Sands rider had playfully put a hole through the guitar of the man standing in the doorway talking to him.

But the crew at the creek did not know that. They opened

up in one ragged roar of gunfire. The puncher at the door swung it shut and dropped the bar, just as the whole night exploded into a fury of sound. Tim blew out the light and each man there jumped to his position at a window.

For one brief moment the Sands riders seemed stunned. The group at the house put spurs to their horses and headed for the ridge, but as they rounded the corner of the house a withering blast of gunfire poured down on them from the ridge.

The riders who survived that wheeled their horses, ran the gantlet of fire from the house and started to retreat the way they had come. But the remainder of their men were fighting clear of the bunkhouse, and they met in a mad tangle halfway between the house and bunkhouse, where they were exposed to the fire from the men on the creek and the men in the barn.

Horses were fighting out there in the night, their shrill screams mingling with the cursing of the men. Already, some of the Sands riders who were afoot had sized up the situation and taken shelter behind downed horses. It was the fire from the creek that they were afraid of, and they turned their attention to it. But the fire from the house took them at their backs, and they soon found that every time they shot they offered a target for the riflemen in the house.

They ceased shooting and firing fell off, and once more darkness settled down. A dozen of these men had taken shelter against the shack, and the men inside could hear them whispering. Seven or eight men out in the tangle of downed horses moved quickly, their talk making a soft murmur in the night.

Tim moved through the living room toward one of the windows. He bumped into the table in the darkness, and he heard the lamp crash over and break. At the window he called:

"Throw down your guns and surrender! You haven't a chance."

For answer, some one shot at the window, and the slug

ripped into the frame beside Tim's head. "Go to hell!" a man shouted. It was the signal for a renewed attack from the men on the creek. The Sands riders, however, did not reply. Tim watched the dark, wondering what they would do. He heard a sudden pounding of feet, and then a shape appeared at the window in front of him. A gun went off almost in his face, and he shot blindly as he wheeled away from the window.

They were storming the house.

Both windows in the front room were swarming with men. It was dangerous in here now, for a man could not tell who he was shooting at. A withering fire from the two windows raked the room, and Tim dropped on his belly. Suddenly someone at the window struck a match and touched it to the curtain. It went up in a bright, licking flare of flame, and by its light Tim saw Jeff lying on the floor against the wall. The men outside saw him, too, for they poured shots in at him. The curtain had burned almost out, and it dropped to the floor, bringing blessed darkness. But only for a second.

It had landed in the oil from the shattered lamp. With a hissing, soughing soft explosion, the oil caught. Tim trained both guns on the window and fired blindly at it. Outside, the men at the creek saw the Sands riders silhouetted in the window, and they opened fire, driving them down.

Tim lunged to his feet and ran into the bedroom. "Better clear out, boys, before this burns on our heads."

Then he turned and called, "Jeff!"

"Yeah." Jeff's old voice was not quite as rumbling as usual.

Tim, in spite of the fire that was licking over half the floor of the room, went over to him. He was lying against the wall, blood pooled under his legs.

"Can you walk?" Tim shouted, for the great wave of gunfire had swelled again. The smoke was filling the room, and the draft through the two shattered windows was fanning the flames.

Jeff shook his head and smiled. "Not unless it's on my hands."

"We got to get out of here, pardner," Tim said. "We'll be fried."

"Go ahead," Jeff said. "I caught one slug too high, son."

Tim looked closely at him and then understood. A fine ribbon of blood was growing at the corner of Jeff's mouth.

"It'll take more than that to down you, old-timer," Tim said softly. He holstered his gun and put both hands under Jeff's arms.

"Don't bother, boy," Jeff murmured. "Hell, git out while you can."

Tim said nothing; he dragged the great bulk of Jeff's body around the fire and into the bedroom. The others had cleared out now, and the window was open. Beyond it he could see the welcome bulk of the bunkhouse, which promised safety.

The light from the fire in the other room made the bedroom almost as light as day. Tim knew the sooner they got out the better, for when the fire broke through the roof and lighted up the night he would have to run a gantlet of gunfire from the riders crouching out there behind their downed horses.

He said to Jeff, "This'll hurt, old-timer."

"You git," Jeff said.

"We git," Tim amended. The table was partially in front of the window. Tim went over and kicked it aside. As he turned, something on the floor caught his eye, and he stopped.

He knelt by it and picked it up. It was the knife that Lugan had kicked there.

It was also the knife with the agate handle! The knife that had been in Borden's throat. Tim took it over to Jeff and knelt by him.

"There's the knife that killed Borden, Jeff," he said.

"Lugan's."

Tim nodded. Old Jeff smiled. "Looks like we let him live a little too long, son."

Tim said nothing, only cursed bitterly. He gathered Jeff in his arms, then, staggering under his great weight, went over to the window. The cross fire in front of it had let up, but it was mostly from his own men. He saw with quiet bitterness that there was already a faint glow of light in the yard. By it he could see the Sands riders crouched behind their horses, and most of them were turned away from the house, their attention on the creek and the bunkhouse.

He sat Jeff on the sill, facing the room, and then squeezed past him out the window, where he crouched against the shack.

"Can you turn around, Jeff, and put your arms over my shoulders?"

"Wait a minute," Jeff said in a tight voice. He tried to move, and gave a great, tight groan, and then did not speak for a moment. "Go on, boy," he whispered. "Leave me."

"You got to, Jeff!" Tim murmured. "You got to!"

"All right."

Jeff heaved himself to his feet, grasping the sill with a grip that made the wood crack. He turned half around and then fell, the upper part of his body hanging out the window.

Tim took both those big arms over his shoulders, rose, got his balance, and started to run.

Immediately, some fool in the bunkhouse gave a yell and said, "Hold it!"

His yell attracted the attention of the Sands riders. Tim was halfway to the end of the bunkhouse when he saw them turn. "Beat 'em down!" he shouted to the men in the bunkhouse. But already the Sands riders began to fire. Tim thought his legs would break with Jeff's great weight on his back. His lungs were almost bursting with the effort, and the bunkhouse seemed to pinwheel slowly in front of his eyes. He kept his eyes on the end of it, his goal, his shelter.

The slugs were kicking up dirt around him now. Beyond

the shadow of the house the night was as light as day by the fire. He was open to anyone who could pick him off.

His pace was slow, infinitesimal. It was like trying to run under water. He felt something whip into his boot tops with such violence that he almost fell. He staggered, caught himself and then something slammed into the calf of his leg, yanking him off balance. He was falling, and there was the bunkhouse ten feet away.

He dug in his heels, driving his legs into the hard dirt. He was going over on his face, but as long as he could get his boots into the dirt he plunged on. There was the end of the bunkhouse, and then the earth rose to hit him in the face. He rolled, then, flinging Jeff off him and around the corner of the bunkhouse. He kept on rolling, rounded the corner, bumped Jeff, staggered to his feet and dragged him the two feet to certain safety against the wall of the bunkhouse.

He knelt there on his hands and knees, gagging for breath, feeling sick. Presently, his breath caught, he crawled over to Jeff and touched him.

"Jeff. Did I hurt like hell?"

Jeff whispered, "Son, you made it, damn it, you made it."

"You're all right now, old-timer. I've got to carry you some more."

"All right."

Tim picked him up and walked the length of the bunkhouse to the window. He could not go in the door, for it was round the other side and in the line of fire. He pounded on the window and it was opened.

"I'll hand him through," Tim said. "Handle him easy, boys."

They lifted Jeff through the window and carried him over to a bunk. At every available opening in the front and end of the bunkhouse there were riflemen. Tim heard one man say, "Just let that fire get good and caught and we'll pick 'em off like quail."

He turned to Jeff and leaned over him. "How is it?" he asked.

"Git in the fight," Jeff whispered. "I'm all right."

"Want water, old-timer?"

"No. Git a gun, son."

Tim turned away; he was feeling all cold inside, for he knew that Jeff would never live out the night. He was hit badly, and even a young man would have had a hard fight to survive it. But old Jeff. Eighty—or maybe ninety—wasn't he? No, it couldn't be done.

Tim went to the window and looked out. Downed horses, almost fifteen of them, lay all around the yard. And behind them were the remaining Sands riders, not more than ten, all told. The terrible toll of that ambush was told mutely in the dozen sprawled riders out in the open, the ones around the base of the house, the five at the far corner of it.

Tim felt a momentary pity for those tough, lost men out there, and then it vanished. They had refused to surrender. They had lived by the gun and chose to die by it. But he would give them another chance.

"Hold it!" he ordered the men in the bunkhouse. They ceased firing, and he called out.

"You haven't got a chance, you men! Give up and you'll stand trial and get justice. Don't and you'll be killed—to a man. Think it over."

They did—for almost ten seconds, and then one shouted, "Come and get us."

"This is the last chance," Tim called. "You can walk out of here to a fair trial. Stay and you'll die!"

There was a long pause. Tim could hear them discussing it, calling to each other. They were not altogether, but scattered around the yard.

Finally their spokesman called. "We fight."

One of the nesters swore and raised his gun, but Tim said, "Wait!"

He turned back to Jeff. His face was taut, and Proctor, looking at him, felt a sudden pity for him. He had the lives of ten men in his hands—rotten lives, it was true, but nevertheless lives.

Tim paused by Jeff. "Did you hear, old-timer?"

"Yeah."

"What can I do?"

Jeff didn't answer for a long time, then he said, "They knew what was doin' when they hired out, son. They'd do it to us—and for money—if they had the chance. We're doin' it to survive."

"But ten men," Tim said quietly. "We can save them."

"Did they save Keith?"

Tim looked at him for a long time, then said in a quiet voice. "All right." He turned and gave the signal to start firing. Again, that roar of gunfire swelled out.

Tim stood there one uncertain moment, then walked toward the back window, climbed out, waited, and ran for the shelter of the barns. His passage went unnoticed by Sands' riders, who were ducked down behind their horses.

At the barn Tim said briefly, "Five of you come with me. Bring your rifles. Climb out of here and one at a time run for the back of the shack. I'll lead off."

He broke away from the barn and streaked for the burning house. His passage did not even draw fire. One by one the other five of them ran for the shack. Now it was between them and the Sands riders. The shack walls had not yet caught, although the roof was ready to fall in.

Tim rounded the north side of the house, his men behind him. When they came to the corner, Tim signaled them to stop, then flattened himself against the wall and peered around the corner. There were the ten men, all bellied down behind the horses which were turned toward the bunkhouse and the creek. The shack itself protected them from the men on the ridge.

Tim took his rifle, and then called out. "Better give up, boys!"

He and his men stepped out into the open, their guns ready. The first Sands rider yanked around at the sound of his voice. He made a wild lunge for the other side of his horse, and someone in the bunkhouse got him. He sprawled grotesquely over the horse's belly.

It seemed to be a signal for the others. They turned their guns on Tim and his men. Tim dropped on his belly and started to shoot.

It was butchery, for now these men had no protection at all. The cross fire of three different points was too much. One rider, more desperate than the others, rose and ran out into the darkness. He got five steps before he went down, tagged by a dozen bullets. One by one, these men were dying.

There were four left. They were hugging the earth, not even bothering to shoot. Tim watched them, forbidding his men to shoot.

Suddenly, one of them waved a bandanna and then stood up, throwing his rifle away. The other three followed suit. They looked tall and haggard and lonely, standing alone on that bloody ground, the crackling fire from the house bringing their faces into bold relief.

Tim walked out toward them, and one by one, the men at the creek, the ridge, the bunkhouse and the corral filed out.

Tim took their guns and turned them over to Will Mersey, and then silently went back into the bunkhouse. Old Jeff was lying there breathing softly, utterly still.

Tim sat down beside him and put his face in his hands. He wondered if he could ever wipe this night from his mind.

"It ain't very pleasant, is it, son?" Jeff whispered.

Tim shook his head.

"I mind the time we ambushed some Utes," Jeff went on slowly. "I slept with it for months. And then I settled it in my mind. It's just this, son. You want peace above all things. But if another man brings war to you, you can only fight. And they brought the war to us, just like them Utes done."

"I reckon," Tim said. For a long while he sat there listening to the sounds out of the night, the sounds of men speaking. There was no laughter, no elation at this victory.

"Tim," Jeff whispered.

"Yeah, old-timer."

"I want to go home."

Tim looked down at him, at his haggard, graying face. "Wait till you're well."

Jeff made a slow, impatient gesture with a hand, then let it drop to his side. "You and me ain't ever fooled each other, Tim. I'm cashin' in my chips. And I want to die on my own land, in my own house—and with my friends."

Tim nodded. There was no use trying to hide it any longer. He wondered if it could be done, and then he knew it could. He knew that old Jeff would hang on until he got home.

"All right, old-timer. I'll fix it up."

All the crew pitched in to help. Lugan's buckboard was bedded down thickly with hay, and Jeff was moved into it and covered with blankets. The men were quiet, for they knew that old Jeff was dying, and that with him would die the salt of the earth, the real old-timer.

So they left the Fish-hook in the dark hours of the night, Will Mersey driving the buckboard team and Tim riding beside it, bound for the Ox-Bow and a place for Jeff to die.

Others were left to finish the job—the job of turning back the sheep now coming down the Tornadoes. There would be no fight there, and they were silently thankful.

19

When dawn broke over the Tornadoes the buckboard was only a mile from the Ox-Bow.

"I'll ride ahead, Will, and have Charlie make ready."

"All right."

Tim lifted his horse into a lope and lined out for the Ox-Bow, already visible in the gray morning.

He rode into the silent yard, dismounted by the live oak and walked toward the house, his head hung in weariness.

He did not know what made him look up. Maybe it was a sound of some sort. But when he did there was Martha standing on the top step.

Tim paused for one brief second, and then Martha came toward him. Afterward, he wondered at what he did—and she did. He took her in his arms and kissed her, and she kissed him.

"Darling, darling," Martha murmured. "I was afraid!"

Tim held her tight. "So was I," he said huskily. "I thought maybe—maybe——"

"Don't say it. It didn't happen," Martha whispered.

"I'll never let you away from me again!" Tim said huskily. "Not even after you're my wife!"

"Not ever," Martha said.

A sound out in the yard made her look up. There was Will in the buckboard. Martha looked at it, and then at Tim, and her look was questioning.

"Jeff got it," Tim said. "There's been a fight, Martha. Sands' men are gone—but they got Jeff."

"Is he alive?"

"Barely."

"I'll go make ready," Martha said.

Will, Tim and Charlie, who was weeping, carried Jeff in the house and put him on the bed. Tim started to undress him, but Jeff opened his eyes and smiled faintly. "Leave the boots on, Tim. Don't undress me. It hurts to move."

They covered him, and Martha sat down beside him. Old Jeff smiled at the sight of her, and stroked her golden hair. Then he motioned Tim to sit beside him.

"I got a couple of things to do yet," Jeff whispered.

"Don't talk, Jeff," Martha said.

"I got to." He looked up at Tim. "At the bank is my will,

Tim. I'm leavin' this place to you and Martha." He paused. "You're gettin' married, ain't you?" he asked simply.

Martha nodded and took Tim's hand. Old Jeff grinned. "That's all I wanted. Now get out of here. I want to sleep."

"But——" Martha began.

"Go on," Jeff said gently. "Everything's all right. I'm happy, girl. I just want to sleep."

Martha kissed him and he smiled. He put his hand out and Tim took it. "So long, old-timer," Tim said.

"Good boy. Good girl," Jeff said. "So long." He closed his eyes. It was Tim who turned at the door and came back to Jeff. He had ceased breathing.

Later that morning St Cloud and Julie rode into the place. Martha ran out to meet them. Julie was radiant. Her face was changed; all of the sulkiness and discontent was gone. She hugged Martha and, laughing, turned to St Cloud.

"I know," Martha said. "I can guess it."

Tim came out then. Julie introduced him to St Cloud, and they shook hands.

Tim looked at Julie, wanting to speak, and Julie realized what he was trying to say.

"You're wondering about Dad, aren't you?" she asked.

"Yes."

Julie took St Cloud's arm. "Maybe I ought to let you say it," she said to St Cloud.

"I'd like to join your fight," St Cloud said to Tim. "Julie, too. You see, we're through with sheep and everything they mean, I reckon. I'd like to help you down Sands."

"You too, Julie?" Tim asked.

Julie nodded gravely. There was quiet defiance in her eyes, but she faced Tim squarely. "You think I'm a rotten daughter to fight against my father?" she asked quietly.

Tim said, "I didn't say it, Julie."

"But you do?"

Tim did not answer.

"Do you know what it means to be loyal to someone for

years and years, hoping against hope that he'll be worth it someday? Do you?"

"No."

"I do," Julie said. "I've hated everything Dad ever did, and the way he did it. I hated the way he put a price on a man and bought him, like he would a valuable ram! I've hated the men he knew, the way he thought, the way he lived! But I was loyal! You can't say I wasn't, can you?"

"No."

"Then can you understand what it meant when I couldn't go on? Do you know what it means to be breathing and walking and eating—and still be dead?"

Tim said nothing.

"Lugan came up to Peavey," Julie went on. "He was going to take me. He was going to hold me until Dad paid him a lot of money. I—I guess it was then I realized it," Julie said, her voice breaking a little bit. "Oh, it was rotten, rotten, all of it!"

"What happened to Lugan?" Tim asked swiftly.

"Dead," St Cloud said briefly.

Tim said quietly, "Do you remember once Julie, you promised to find the man who killed Borden?"

"I think Dad did now," Julie said bitterly.

"It was Lugan," Tim said. He brought out the big knife and showed it to her. "I found that in his shack." He told them of what had happened last night, of the fight at Lugan's. Julie and St Cloud heard him out gravely.

"Then Sands is through," St Cloud said. "Through with you, I mean." His voice was edged with iron. "He isn't through with me, though."

"He'll leave," Tim said. "He's licked."

"I'll find him," St Cloud said. "When I do there's somethin' I want to say to him, somethin' that's been waitin' to be said for some years now."

"You won't hurt him, will you?" Julie asked, looking up at him.

"No. Not the way you think. But I'll hurt him another way," St Cloud said quietly.

Martha took Julie's arm and went into the house. In the kitchen, Charlie, his face impassive as ever, had their breakfast waiting.

After he had put it on the table he went out. He was like a dog who has lost his master, and Tim felt a great pity for him. He had served out most of his life in old Jeff Hardy's service, and now he was alone.

While they ate, St Cloud told them of what had happened at Peavey. Martha supplemented it. They were talking about the sheep when Charlie appeared at the door.

"Someone coming," he announced.

Tim rose and went to the door. Down the road a lone horseman was approaching. Tim watched him a long time, and when he was sure he turned to Julie and said, "It's your father."

St Cloud came to the door. "It's him, all right," he said. He stepped out, and Julie brushed past Tim at the door. The four of them waited under the live oak tree, Julie and St Cloud a little ahead of Tim and Martha while Sands rode over the bridge and pulled up in front of them. His face was haggard, lined by a gnawing disappointment that was most evident in his eyes.

He looked first at Julie and then at St Cloud, and his eyes were hard, arrogant. Then his gaze shifted to Tim. "I'm beaten," he said. "I'm leaving the Basin."

"All right," Tim said.

"Come, Julie," Sands said. "I think they'll lend you a horse."

"I'm not coming," Julie said quietly.

Sands looked steadily at her. "I think you are," he said. "We're leaving." He smiled slightly, almost kindly. "For St Louis this time."

"She's not goin' with you," St Cloud said. "She won't say it, Sands, but I will. She's through with you and your murderin' ways—forever."

Sands' glance shuttled back to Julie. "Is that true?"

Julie only nodded.

"Another thing that won't make you happy," St Cloud said. "Julie and I are gettin' married."

Sands was still looking at Julie. "Is that true, too?"

"Yes," Julie said.

"You mean you want to marry—him?"

"Yes, isn't it queer?" Julie said bitterly, softly. "He only loves me, Dad. And I love him. He hasn't got your kind of ambition; he doesn't murder people. He doesn't want to own a hundred square miles of land. He'd like to be honest and friendly, not feared. He'd like to have people respect him, not for his money and his power, but for himself." She paused. "Isn't that queer, I say?"

"But he's a cheap gunman," Sands said quietly.

"*Was,* you mean," St Cloud said.

Sands did not even look at him; he was watching Julie. "I give you one more chance to tell me that you aren't sincere," Sands said slowly. "Did you mean what you said?"

"Every bit of it," Julie said firmly.

"Then I'm afraid your husband will spend the rest of his life in jail," Sands said calmly. "Are you aware that I never hire a man unless he has warrants out for him somewhere? Do you think I'll let you marry that—that trash, and not turn him over to the law?"

"I'll serve whatever prison sentence is comin' to me," St Cloud said quietly. "We've got that settled. It won't be much of a sentence, though. I killed a man who tried to kill me. His friends were in the county offices. They ain't now. I think I may get out of it without a trial."

"You forget that you've done some work for me," Sands said dryly.

"And you forget you ain't got a witness alive to prove it," St Cloud answered.

Martha said calmly, "Sands, you talk as if you were still free to plunder and kill, like you've done in the past."

"Do you see any sheriff arresting me?" Sands answered arrogantly.

"If you don't clear out of here one will do it," Tim said thickly. "We're tryin' to save Julie the experience of watchin' her father swing from a cottonwood tree. But you talk about ten minutes longer and I think we'll all change our minds."

"Yes," Julie said swiftly. "Go on, Dad! Go on while you can! I've stuck by you as long as I could—longer than I could! We're finished! Can't you understand? We're finished!"

Sands smiled bleakly. "I have a letter here in my coat that I brought up from Rincon, St Cloud," he said. "It's from a U.S. marshal. I think you'll be interested."

He raised a hand to the inside pocket of his coat. Then, with a move as quick as the flick of a whip, he yanked a gun out of a shoulder holster and leveled it at the four of them.

"Don't move, any of you!" he said swiftly. His glance raised to Tim. "There's one slug in this gun for you, Enever. But the first one is going to be spent on St Cloud. I think I can kill him and still kill you."

None of them said anything. Martha caught her breath in a little moan of dismay.

"Julie," Sands said, "step away from—your husband."

"If you kill him I'll kill myself," Julie said quietly.

"He won't kill me," St Cloud said calmly. "He thinks too much of his hide."

That was a mistake, Tim saw. He saw it immediately in the way Sands' eyes smeared over. He knew that it was only a matter of seconds before Sands would shoot. And then it came to him swiftly, came to him just as plainly as if St Cloud had said to him, "Tim, you've got a gun on your right hip. Julie is standin' in front of you, and a little to the side of you, and there's a space of three inches between her and me. I'm goin' to rawhide Sands until he's mad and lookin' only at me. Then make your play. Make it fast and make it good, because it's our only chance."

Sands said, "Damn you for a helpless fool, St Cloud!" His thumb settled on the hammer, ready to pull it back.

"You're yellow," St Cloud taunted. "Enever knows you're yellow." And then he said it as plainly as it could be said, without telling Sands. "If Enever made a pass at his gun you'd drop that iron, Sands. You're too yellow to shoot."

Sands' eyes were a blazing fury.

It was then that Tim acted. His hand was hanging at his side. He streaked it up, picking his gun up on the way, and when it was little more than hip high he let it off.

He was looking at Sands, not at the space between St Cloud's and Julie's arm. He saw Sands shudder under the drive of that bullet. He saw out of the corner of his eye that St Cloud had melted to the ground. He heard Sands' gun go off a split second later.

And he raised his gun and emptied it at Sands. It drove Sands out of the saddle, and he fell in a limp heap, dead before he hit the ground.

St Cloud rose and held his arms out and Julie was in them, great sobs racking her body. Over her shoulder, St Cloud smiled his thanks.

Tim looked at his gun and threw it away from him, and then looked at Martha.

"Yes, we're through with that now, Tim. Through forever," Martha said.

About the Author

LUKE SHORT, whose real name was Frederick D. Glidden, was born in Illinois in 1907 and died in 1975. He wrote nearly fifty books about the West and was a winner of the special Western Heritage Trustee Award. Before devoting himself to writing westerns, he was a trapper in the Canadian Subarctic, worked as an assistant to an archeologist and was a newsman. Luke Short believed an author could write best about the places he knows most intimately, so he usually located his westerns on familiar ground. He lived with his wife in Aspen, Colorado.